SPECIAL MESSAGE TO READERS

THE ULVERSCROFT FOUNDATION
(registered UK charity number 264873)

was established in 1972 to provide funds for research, diagnosis and treatment of eye diseases. Examples of major projects funded by the Ulverscroft Foundation are:-

- The Children's Eye Unit at Moorfields Eye Hospital, London
- The Ulverscroft Children's Eye Unit at Great Ormond Street Hospital for Sick Children
- Funding research into eye diseases and treatment at the Department of Ophthalmology, University of Leicester
- The Ulverscroft Vision Research Group, Institute of Child Health
- Twin operating theatres at the Western Ophthalmic Hospital, London
- The Chair of Ophthalmology at the Royal Australian College of Ophthalmologists

You can help further the work of the Foundation by making a donation or leaving a legacy. Every contribution is gratefully received. If you would like to help support the Foundation or require further information, please contact:

THE ULVERSCROFT FOUNDATION
**The Green, Bradgate Road, Anstey
Leicester LE7 7FU, England
Tel: (0116) 236 4325**

website: www.foundation.ulverscroft.com

A RATIONAL PROPOSAL

When Verity Bowman's uncle dies, she discovers that she's inherited his fortune — as well as his attorney, Charles Congreve. But there's a catch. Concerned that Verity would be tempted to give herself completely to frivolity, her uncle has stipulated that she must first prove to have spent six months 'in a wholly rational manner'. As Charles oversees the conditions of the will, he realises he's falling in love with Verity — but his social position precludes marriage to a wealthy heiress. Can they find a way to make a life together?

Books by Jan Jones
in the Linford Romance Library:

FAIRLIGHTS
AN ORDINARY GIFT
ONLY DANCING
A QUESTION OF THYME
AN UNCONVENTIONAL ACT

JAN JONES

A RATIONAL PROPOSAL

The Furze House Irregulars

Complete and Unabridged

LINFORD
Leicester

First published in Great Britain in 2018

First Linford Edition
published 2019

A catalogue record for this book is available
from the British Library.

ISBN 978–1–4448–4131–2

A Rational Proposal

is dedicated to the incomparable
Georgette Heyer. None of us would
be writing Regencies without you

Dramatis Personae

in order of appearance (mostly)

Charles Congreve — attorney, younger son of good family
[Previously in, *The Kydd Inheritance, An Unconventional Act*]
Verity Bowman — recipient of an unexpected bequest
Anne Bowman — Verity's widowed mother
(James Harrington — Anne Bowman's brother, admiral, deceased)
(John Bowman — Verity's half-brother from her father's first marriage)
(Selina Bowman — John's wife, increasing)
(Reverend Milsom — an encroaching parson)
Mr Tweedie — Charles's senior partner
[Previously in *The Kydd Inheritance, Fair Deception, An Unconventional Act*]

Jenny Prettyman — Verity's friend
[Previously in *An Unconventional Act*]

Adam Prettyman — landowner and retired actor
[Previously in *Fair Deception,*
An Unconventional Act]

(Alexander & Caroline Rothwell — politician and horse trainer respectively)
[Previously in *Fair Deception,*
Fortunate Wager,
(*An Unconventional Act*)]

Julia Congreve — Charles's sister, Verity's best friend, beauty, knows everyone

Mrs Congreve — Charles's mother, Verity's godmother

Lieutenant Crisp — pleasant young officer

Lieutenant Neville — not-so-pleasant young officer

Lilith Fitzgilbert — scholar, Julia & Verity's friend

Benedict Fitzgilbert — baron, head of the Pool, Charles's friend, Lilith's brother

Nicholas Dacre — rake, horse racing enthusiast, member of the Pool

Kitty Eastwick — Verity's runaway half-sister from her father's first marriage

Captain Simon Eastwick — Kitty's husband, very busy gentleman indeed

Molly Turner — seamstress and occasional lady of the night

Fred Grimes — hackney driver

Sir Philip Munro — baronet thief-taker, smitten with Julia

Susan Norris — former lady's maid

Hannah — former kitchen servant

Various attorneys, clerks, maids, footmen, shopkeepers, officers, ladies who socialise, street children and ruffians

1

Kennet End, Newmarket,
October 1817

Miss Verity Bowman, undoubtedly by design, was looking particularly fetching, framed in the window seat of the dower house wearing a demure black mourning gown. Only the cut of the material and the subtle sheen of the satin gave away the fact that it had come from one of the more exclusive establishments on Bond Street.

Charles Congreve appreciated the picture she presented, fully understood why her uncle had made her his heir, and desired nothing more than to strangle the pair of them. Sadly, there was little to be gained in strangling a man who had departed this earth just ten days since. In addition, the legal brotherhood tended to look askance at those of their members who took to throttling clients. Which, he was very much afraid, Verity was about to become.

Unaware of these less than affable thoughts, Verity smiled warmly as he took a seat. 'Charles, how lovely. Such an age since we have seen you. Mama and I are so glad it is you dealing with this sad business, though I do hope nothing very dreadful has happened to poor Mr Tweedie?'

Verity had happened to poor Mr Tweedie. Charles's senior partner had taken one appalled look at the codicil appended to Admiral Harrington's will (a document that had been perfectly sound in wind and limb when it had left his own chambers), made an astringent remark about amateur notaries in Newmarket, and announced himself to be at a delicate stage with several cases, too much so to travel into Suffolk to undertake the process of winding up the late admiral's affairs. He was confident Charles would manage.

'Thank you,' Charles had replied, feeling anything but grateful. 'You have recollected Miss Bowman is my mother's goddaughter and a particular friend of my sister?'

Mr Tweedie had looked at him over the rim of his spectacles. 'Naturally. A family attorney never forgets anything. Nor, as I am sure I do not need to remind you, does he allow personal considerations to influence his judgement. I repeat, I repose complete confidence in whatever decisions you might find yourself making. You had best leave directly after the funeral.'

So now Charles murmured his partner's excuses, was pressed to take tea and macaroons, and his portmanteau was carried up to a guest bedroom just as if he was an invited visitor and not a common attorney. And all he could think of was how far Verity's intelligent blue eyes were going to widen when he broke the terms of Admiral Harrington's will to her. And then how far they would narrow. And how he had rarely, if ever, managed to get the upper hand of her in all their dealings together.

Ah well, there was nothing to be gained in shuffling around the matter. The sooner the business was concluded, the sooner he could be on his way. Charles cleared his throat and addressed Verity's mother. 'You will be glad to hear, Mrs Bowman, that we laid your brother to rest in sufficient style for his calling and with a large number of mourners in the funeral party, all of them decently and respectfully arrayed.'

'Thank you,' said Anne Bowman in a low voice. 'It seems dreadfully wrong, losing James this suddenly, and doubly cruel, coming just as we were able to offer him a settled home whenever his interests brought him to Newmarket. Such a vital man, always.'

Vital was one word for it. Energetic, opinionated and meddlesome were others. A complete contrast to his sister, although Mrs Bowman did seem less crushed and faded than Charles remembered her from previous years.

He gave a professionally encouraging smile. 'The admiral impressed me as a very industrious man. He must have been a fine officer to serve under. Many crew members from his past ships were at the funeral and they all said as much. He had, of necessity, a roving life until very recently, but he was fully sensible of your kindness in extending the invitation to reside here whenever his affairs permitted it. He has directed us to purchase a lifetime annuity for you in order to increase the comfort your coming years. It will effectively double your income.'

Verity clasped her mother's hand and turned a glowing face to Charles that momentarily robbed him of speech. 'Oh, that is good news! How very thoughtful of my uncle. And it will be forever, Mama. The income will not be dependent on your remaining single, as Papa's niggardly jointure is.'

Charles sipped his tea, arranging his

phrasing. 'As I understand it, the admiral was particularly concerned to make reparation for what he considered to be a lack of flexibility in the late Mr Bowman's dispositions.'

Verity lifted her chin. 'You mean Uncle James disapproved of the unfair way Papa left everything to John, cut Kitty and me out completely apart from my settlement that he could do nothing about, and allowed Mama a pittance and the right to reside in this dreary house, only if she remained a widow?'

As these had been almost word-for-word the admiral's sentiments, Charles had to temper his reply. 'Miss Bowman, you know it would be most improper for me to be drawn on such a topic.'

'I keep forgetting,' she said unrepentantly. 'Poor Charles. It must be very trying, being discreet all the time.'

'As your uncle's executor,' he said, hanging on to formality by a hair's breadth, 'I can tell you that to mitigate your own situation, he has left the remainder of his estate to you.' Blast the chit. Now he'd blurted it out without any preparation of what was to follow. He took refuge in the contents of his plate.

Verity's eyes widened just as he'd prophesied. 'Uncle James has left his money to me? To me, Charles?'

'After the annuity for your mother has been taken out, yes. He considered the senior branch of the Harrington family to have sufficient for their purposes.'

'Goodness, I don't imagine that pleased them.'

Charles's precarious gravity wavered. 'I have attended more harmonious readings of the will.'

The late Admiral Harrington's parents and older brother hadn't quite seen the loss of his considerable prize money in the same light. There had been remarkably high words spoken. Charles needed another moment to recover his equilibrium, remembering the uncharacteristic grave delight with which his senior partner had read out the terms of the will. No love lost there, despite Tweedie & Tweedie having been the family's legal advisers from time immemorial. 'You are his niece,' he said.

'I am. And it is true that the merest mention of Grandmother Harrington and my eldest uncle were enough to drive Uncle James to the brandy decanter. I am simply so used to everything going to John, I forget he and Kitty are only Mama's step-children and thus not related to the Harringtons at all. This is wonderful, Charles. May I be practical? How much will it bring in?'

'We will not know the exact figure until your uncle's outstanding accounts are settled. I shall begin work on those on my return to town. However, I would be remiss in my duty if I did not inform you that there are . . . conditions on your bequest.'

'Conditions?'

Under that bright scrutiny, Charles shifted in his seat. He glanced at his plate but the macaroons had been eaten and the tea drunk. He had neglected to take small bites, as Mr Tweedie always advised, should prevarication be required during an awkward conversation. Rather basely, he put this oversight down to Verity's account too.

He cleared his throat. 'Admiral Harrington was concerned a sudden acquisition of wealth might cause you to give yourself completely to frivolity. According to a frankly amateurish codicil that I assure you neither Mr Tweedie nor I knew anything about, he had seen some evidence for this belief on a visit he made here during the summer. To counteract such tendencies, you must prove you have spent six months in a wholly rational manner before anything more than pin money can be released to you.'

Verity gave a peal of laughter. 'I am to read my Bible for half-an-hour every morning before breakfast, is that it?'

Despite himself, Charles smiled.

'Would your uncle consider that rational?'

'He would not. He nearly came to blows with Reverend Milsom on his last visit because the silly man had chosen *The Storm At Sea* as his sermon and tied in a great many unlikely occurrences, finishing with the pouring of oil on troubled water, all of which my uncle as a naval man took exception to. What the vicar was really after was to tell John and Farmer Quigley they shouldn't quarrel over the fishpond, but it was all for nothing as John was unwell so did not attend church. Even if he had, he would have had no idea that the sermon was directed at him.'

'Miss Bowman, you are incorrigible.'

She flashed a smile at him. 'Dearest Charles, do please stop calling me *Miss Bowman*. I keep thinking you have taken me in dislike.'

'I am here as your uncle's man of business, Verity. I am soon to be your own. A little formality is in order.'

'Nonsense. One cannot be formal

with a person one has known since the cradle. Tell me what I must do. How absurd of Uncle James to make such a condition. It must have been when here was here for the July meeting, do you not think, Mama? But if he *will* arrive when we are doing our best to make the most of the grimmest summer weather I can remember, what does he expect? We so rarely go out for our own amusement otherwise.'

'I believe he wished to ensure that you are not as empty-headed as you occasionally pretend,' said Charles drily.

Verity sighed. 'It is the sad lot of women to be misunderstood by their menfolk. I have often remarked it.'

'Yet you did nothing to countermand your uncle's impression of your character?'

'Had I known it was wanted, I would have done,' said Verity, looking vexed. 'But how was I to discover it? Your own excellent family may encourage conversation, Charles, but Papa preferred

11

docility in his womenfolk. He did not like Mama and me discussing events taking place in the wider world. We were supposed to sit in silent admiration and take our opinions from him. One would think we had never learnt to read and were not competent to peruse a newspaper on our own.'

Charles winced. She had painted an accurate picture of many of the families who gave Mr Tweedie their patronage. He deplored the attitude but had never sought to change it for fear of losing their business. Perhaps he should not be so circumspect in the future.

Verity continued, 'You forget how comparatively little we have seen of Uncle James. It is only these last six months that he has been able to stay with us. He liked to talk of his travels, and of matters in town and around the rest of the world. Mama was so happy to have him here, after years of his not visiting due to not getting on with Papa, that I did not want to upset his mood by saying anything out of place. I should have followed my instincts. Let me refill your cup, Charles. Would you like a piece of this plum cake? It is very good. John and Selina have imported a French chef on purpose to be the sensation of the neighbourhood, so Mama and I had no difficulty in enticing Cook across the park to look after us here. Very fortunately, it was before Selina discovered M'sieur Gaston has trouble with the plain everyday fare John prefers.'

Charles could not repress a chuckle. 'You are a wicked young woman, Verity. I pity your eventual husband.'

'Envy him, you mean,' said Verity, supremely confident. 'I shall arrange our domestic affairs so he will think it pure chance that he is so comfortable. If I marry at all, that is.' She tilted her head to one side. 'Have we finished the examination? Do you believe me to be intelligent and not a flibbertigibbet?'

'Verity . . . ' protested Mrs Bowman.

'I always did,' said Charles. 'But it is not what I *believe* that is important.

The difficulty lies in *proving* you have spent six months in a rational manner. The senior Harrington branch will undoubtedly mount a challenge else.'

'I see. To whom am I to prove it?'

Charles felt himself colouring. 'To me. As I am your uncle's executor, you inherit me along with his fortune.'

Verity's face melted into a wry, amused smile. 'And you are far too honourable to hand it over with anything less than a commendation that would stand up in fifteen courts of law. My poor Charles, how very shabby of Uncle James.'

Until now, these had also been Charles's feelings, but the tea and cake had mellowed him. 'I daresay it will not be so very onerous. I shall give the matter some thought. Mrs Bowman, will you excuse me? I have sat here long enough in all my dirt and should like to wash off the dust of the journey. Also, I must pen a note to my friend Prettyman at Fordham, apprising him of my intention to call tomorrow. There

14

is a matter of an expiring lease to settle that Mr Tweedie has asked me to oversee while I am in the neighbourhood.'

'Oh, may I come with you?' said Verity at once. 'We can use Mama's carriage. I have not seen Jenny this fortnight at least.' She tapped his hand playfully. 'And while we are there, I shall enquire in a most serious manner about the progress of their repairs to the Prior's Ground. Is that rational enough for you?'

Charles hesitated. He had not foreseen this. 'It is, and I cannot bar you from making a call in your own equipage, but I will be discussing business, Verity.'

She smiled sunnily. 'And Jenny and I shall be playing with the children while we search for meat in the local gossip. I perfectly understand. You need not fear you will be expected to dance attendance on me.'

And there was the reward for his labours gone, reflected Charles glumly as he followed a footman up the stairs. The worst of it was, he did not quite see how Verity had done it. He had intended a night's stop here only, to acquaint the ladies with the terms of Admiral Harrington's will. That should have been ample time to advance them a sum if it was needed, get the papers signed and witnessed, come to an agreement on what constituted rational behaviour, *not* be drawn into any of Verity's more far-fetched schemes, and then he would be away to Rooke Hall for a couple of days of relaxation with Adam Prettyman.

Prettyman was a comparatively new acquaintance, but they had straight-away recognised in each other a kindred spirit. Both were younger sons who had chosen to work for a living outside their natural milieu rather than grub on the family estate for little more than board and lodging. Both were active men, preferring a busy life to wasting hours in idle pursuits. True, Adam had solved his early restlessness in a rather extreme manner by becoming the actor-manager of a company of players, whereas Charles had settled for studying the law, with side excursions into protecting people's rights in person where the law seemed inadequate, but essentially they were alike. They shared the difficulty of having feet in two worlds, of matching their persona to the current situation. With Adam's retirement from the stage, Charles had aided his friend's re-integration into society by introducing him to the fencing and boxing saloons he favoured in town. In return, Adam was one of the few people in whose presence Charles didn't have to think about who he was, attorney or gentleman. Verity had been more correct than she knew when she'd made that light-hearted comment about the nature of his work being trying for him. Charles was as thick-skinned as any other man who'd spent his formative years at Eton, but at times the distinction between his two lives was damnable. He had been looking forward to two or three days at Rooke Hall where he could simply be himself.

Now he was committed to a morning visit only and back here to sleep a second night. It was, he told himself, the last time he would underestimate Verity Bowman. She might be the very picture of an empty-headed ninny when she chose, but as she had reminded him earlier, he had known her since the cradle. Behind that amiable facade, Verity was as nimble-witted as a whole shipful of monkeys. He would do well to remember it. Starting, he rather thought, with dinner this evening.

2

Her own money. As Charles left the room, Verity's thoughts were alive with new possibilities. She had known Uncle James would help with Mama's future comfort, for he had said so when he visited after Papa's death. It had never occurred to her that she herself might benefit. Foremost in her mind was the significant circumstance that depending upon the size of the bequest, she might not now have to marry in order to live comfortably. She would be able to support herself rather than depend on the whims of a husband.

Verity had no great opinion of the married state. Some of her friends seemed happy, but others appeared very little better off than when they had been living under their father's roof. Additionally, Mama was so much more content as a widow, and their lives so much less proscribed that, apart from the finances, she could not see why matrimony should be thought desirable. It was thus more important than ever to keep Charles here for a few days, to impress upon him her sobriety so she might command her own affairs sooner rather than later. She opened her mouth to observe as much when her mother gave a tiny sigh.

'It is a shame George Tweedie did not come himself. I would have liked to welcome him here.'

Verity looked at her mother, surprised. 'Mr Tweedie, Mama? I was thinking Charles would be far more amenable to our notions of wresting your dowager's pittance away from John's control.'

'I am sure he will do so in handsome style, my dear, but I assure you George Tweedie is a most dogged man. You have only met him once or twice. I saw a great deal of him in former times. He was at school with your uncle many years ago, though he was older of course, and his family has always acted for the Harringtons. It was he who drew up my marriage articles. He was so unobtrusive and thoughtful of my comfort during the process. His restful presence was one of the few blessings in a very turbulent period.'

Verity hid her startled reaction to this confidence. Mama had often recounted episodes from her childhood, but she'd rarely mentioned the time immediately before her marriage. It was not so very surprising, perhaps. She was in general so quiet and reflective, that the bustle of a betrothal and wedding must have been very trying to her sensibilities. Verity tried to imagine her grandparents getting up grand schemes for the entertainment of the wedding party. No, they were all correctness and show. Their eldest son was exactly in their image, so how they had produced her loud, rumbustious Uncle James, who had always said what he thought at the moment he thought it, she had no idea.

'Then we must certainly invite Mr

Tweedie to visit us when he is not so busy. Oh . . . ' She jumped up, having caught a glimpse of a visitor advancing up the dower house path. 'Mama, you don't wish to see Reverend Milsom, do you? Shall I give orders that we are not to be disturbed?'

She whisked out into the passage before her mother could answer and hissed instructions to the footman.

'There,' she said, re-entering the room. 'I declare that man must have spies the length of the village. No sooner does he hear that a visitor from London has bespoke the gig from the Horseshoes than he hastens up here to find out why.'

'I daresay he would not have stayed so very long,' said Mama.

'Long enough to cut up our peace,' said Verity, keeping a covert eye on the window. 'And now the wretched man is heading across the park to John and Selina. How long do you suppose it will be before we are favoured with a visit from *them*?'

'John will be about the estate at this time of the day,' said her mother peaceably. 'Selina will no doubt be resting.'

'This is true. She is certainly making the most of her interesting condition. Reverend Milsom will have a wasted walk which is only what he deserves.' A small smile played around Verity's mouth. 'All the same, Mama, these constant interferences in our business are becoming somewhat wearisome. I begin to have a little idea . . . '

Mrs Bowman regarded her daughter with a wariness that showed she was not quite so gentle and passive as others often thought her. 'Am I to know what it is?'

Verity smiled as the beauty of her plan unfolded in her head. 'Oh yes, and I think you will like it.'

★　★　★

Verity might be playing a game with him, but Charles still found pleasure in

23

escorting the two ladies through from the saloon to the small dining room. He suspected extra dishes had been added to the spread on the table to cater for a gentleman's appetite which made it a far cry from his bachelor dinners at home. He intended to do full justice to the excellent cooking.

He helped them all to portions of chicken in a butter sauce and said conversationally, 'I did not know you had recently been in town.'

'We have not,' said Verity. 'Why would you think so?'

'That gown did not come from Bury St Edmunds.'

She stroked the rich satin with a roguish smile. 'No indeed. I had it made up in Bond Street for John and Selina's wedding.'

Charles was taken aback. 'You wore black to your brother's wedding? That seems rather singular, even if you have little love for him.'

Verity and her mother exchanged amused glances. 'You would not know the circumstances as you did not act for my father. Unless you have been talking to Julia?'

'I frequently talk to Julia,' said Charles. 'It is the fastest way to find out what is going on in town. About what, particularly?'

'John's wedding. Oh no, I remember she was away at the time or we would have called.'

'Verity,' said Charles, exasperated.

She flashed an engaging smile at him. 'I beg your pardon. The facts are simply that Selina, having been modestly indecisive about marriage these past two years, accepted John within moments of learning Papa had left him Kennet End without even Mama and me as distraints upon his purse. I promise you, Charles, *within moments*. In one breath she was commiserating with us prettily on our loss and saying how she couldn't bear the thought of John's broad shoulders having to support the burden of the estate alone, and in the next breath she was accepting the situation of loving helpmeet and arranging a mutually convenient time to visit the foremost goldsmith in Bury St Edmunds for the purpose of choosing a ring. She was then overcome with remorse at having kept John dangling for so long. It was very affecting, was it not, Mama? She fixed on an early, very quiet, wedding at St George's, Hanover Square because our period of mourning had barely started and she did not wish to offend the sensibilities of the district. So noble of her, do you not think?'

Charles shook with laughter. 'You are a wicked young woman, Verity. Your brother's wife is a sensitive lady, I apprehend.'

'Can you doubt it?' Verity ate a couple of mouthfuls of the chicken. 'Clearly my provincial mourning dresses would never do to celebrate such an auspicious occasion so, as we had been invited to stay with her well-connected cousins in town, I thought it safest to visit the same modiste as Selina and charge my wedding finery to John's account.'

Charles regained his composure with some difficulty. 'Do remind me never to annoy you.'

She opened her eyes wide. 'I was not annoyed in the least. As I explained to John, it was a compliment to my new sister-in-law, designed to show how much I trusted her taste and judgement. He must have agreed, for he didn't argue the outlay at all.'

'You are a minx.'

'But a nicely dressed one, you have to admit.'

Charles was betrayed into another smile and didn't even begrudge her the tiny curve of her lips in triumph at having coaxed him into a better humour. That was the other thing he had forgotten, that despite the outrageous scrapes she and Julia had often required rescuing from, Verity herself was never less than amusing to be with. The danger lay in encouraging her.

Accordingly, he turned to his hostess.

'I am glad to see you in good looks, Mrs Bowman,' he said. 'Forgive me, I should have mentioned it as soon as I arrived, but you basely distracted me with those excellent macaroons.'

He spoke nothing but the truth regarding Mrs Bowman's looks, yet she was still a water-colour painting compared to Verity's vivid oils. It was difficult to credit Mr Tweedie's assertion earlier this week that over twenty years ago, Miss Anne Harrington had been the prettiest girl in the county and much in demand as a dance partner.

'As pretty as her brother was handsome,' he'd said, sitting at his desk in unaccustomed stillness with the admiral's problematical will in this hands. 'We have always had a number of clients in Suffolk, so I saw a good deal of them, being the junior partner myself in those days and thus the one to be sent whenever something needed dealing with.'

'My commiserations,' said Charles pointedly.

'It was the tragedy that changed her. You would have been too young to remember.'

'I should think I was. Twenty years ago I was still in the schoolroom. What happened?'

'Long before he made Admiral, James Harrington had a friend William Lawrence. One saw them everywhere, they were up to all the rigs and rows in town. Both James and Anne were cut from a different cloth to their parents and elder brother. Anne had a *tendre* for Will Lawrence who was lively and witty, and as darkly dashing as the Harringtons were fair. Will and Anne had an understanding but his prospects depended on his grandmother, so he would not declare himself in public until he had been to see the old lady to discover what she might do for them.'

'That seems most correct. Did she disapprove? Was that the tragedy?'

'Alas, we never knew what she would have thought. James Harrington was under orders to join his ship. Will

29

Lawrence travelled down to Portsmouth with him, saw him safely away, then set off to visit his grandmother. He was held up by highwaymen and killed on the turnpike en route. It was a shocking thing, quite terrible. The joy went out of Anne Harrington like a . . . like a chandelier with all the candles snuffed at the same instant.'

Charles felt a moment of pure astonishment at his prosaic partner's sudden incursion into poetry. 'A tragedy indeed,' he said. 'Were the perpetrators caught?'

'No. Anne took it very hard. Too hard, in my opinion. Mr Bowman was a widower who had been pressing his suit with her parents. She had been keeping him at arm's length, as she had everyone, but with Lawrence gone, she simply couldn't put up a fight any more. I was involved in drawing up the marriage articles for her father, principally to ensure her portion would be settled on her own children rather than those from

Bowman's previous marriage, and I never saw such a pale, wan bride. I know James Harrington considered it a shabby thing for his sister to do, so soon after Will Lawrence's death, but there you are. He was at sea; there was no one at home to counsel her otherwise and it wasn't my place to say anything. All I could do was tie up her settlement as tightly as I knew how. From my knowledge of her, it troubled me greatly that Bowman wasn't a warmer man, but an offer is an offer and she was under considerable pressure from her parents. Do give her my best wishes. She will always be a beautiful woman in my eyes.'

Charles did so, being rewarded with a lightening of Mrs Bowman's expression and a smiling message to take back, although he wasn't sure he'd agree with her description of his rather fussy senior partner as a dear sweet man. He turned the talk to whether they had any plans to improve the dower house.

'Pull it down and start again?' said Verity. 'This time without the cramped rooms, mean windows and high ceilings? Papa's ancestor must have nursed a truly remarkable hatred for his mother. The only nice features at all are the front bays and they were added later.'

'It is a very trying building,' murmured Mrs Bowman.

Verity put her head on one side. 'Dearest Charles,' she said in a coaxing voice, 'if we put our incomes together, could Mama and I afford to take a house somewhere else? There are some nice properties in Newmarket itself, towards the London road. Furze House has been free this past month, though it is somewhat run down and may need a little work. This one is so gloomy, as well as being too close to John and Selina. I am not sure I *can* be rational here. It simply cries out for gaiety and frivolity as an antidote to being crushed.'

Charles looked at her with horror.

The prospect of Verity setting up an independent establishment, even with her mother, especially in a house that *needed a little work,* filled him with the liveliest unease. John Bowman might be a loud, pompous, self-important bore, but at least his presence across the park was some sort of brake on his half-sister's wilder schemes.

★ ★ ★

The next morning, Charles gazed with wry appreciation at the array of breakfast dishes laid out on the sideboard. It seemed Verity wasn't finished yet. He filled his plate and mentally braced himself for the next idea she had in mind to spring on him.

Early morning, however, appeared to be sacrosanct as far as assaults on his better judgement were concerned. Verity made sensible, cheerful conversation whilst not troubling to hide a hearty appetite, and was ready to leave the house in half the time his sister Julia usually managed. She reminded her mother not to agree to anything John and Selina might suggest should they visit, nor to mention Uncle James's money, and then settled herself neatly on the carriage seat opposite Charles as the coachman gave the horses the off.

'Yes?' he said.

She chuckled. 'I do like an intelligent man. Such a relief after living with Papa and John. Charles, I have been giving some thought to my uncle's bequest. The wording, as you say, is awkward. Nice as it is to have you here, I daresay you would not find it very convenient to live in the dower house with us for the next six months in order to continually observe my behaviour.'

A lesser man might have shuddered. 'It would be most *in*convenient,' he said repressively.

She nodded with a satisfaction that increased his alarm. 'I thought as much. I believe I have come up with a solution that will suit us both.'

He took a guarded breath. 'Yes?'

She smiled at him. 'In the interests of following a rational programme of which my uncle would approve, I propose that Mama and I should remove to London with you.'

3

Charles choked and needed recourse to the large handkerchief his companion considerately handed him before he could answer. 'Verity, you will be the death of me. Now I understand that handsome breakfast. What have you in mind to do in London that is so much more rational than following an improving programme of reading or some such here?'

'Many things. Charles, you have *seen* the dower house. It positively invites one to kick against it. London has well-stocked libraries. London has galleries and museums. London has those scientific lectures you were telling us about yesterday. They sound most interesting.'

Charles silently cursed himself for a fool. 'I will send you the transcripts.'

Small blue demons danced in Verity's

eyes as she folded her hands demurely in her lap. 'I also thought I might go about with you, Charles. Then there can be no question of not spending my time in a rational manner, for I am sure you do nothing that is not sensible and sober.'

Charles did many things that were neither sensible nor sober, and he had no intention of enlightening Verity about them. The very thought made his blood run cold. 'Leaving aside the small difficulty that the majority of my daylight hours are spent working, you, your mother and your maids will never fit into my bachelor quarters in the Albany.'

'How ridiculous you are. We will stay with Godmama, of course. She wrote to invite us some time ago. She won't mind at all.'

'It is a dreadful idea, Verity. Julia is hardly the companion to aid you in a pursuit of rationality. I don't believe I have seen her with a book in her hands since she left school.' He thought back.

'Possibly not even then.'

Verity's eyes flickered for a moment. 'Dearest Julia. She will help me when I explain. Besides, I wish to extract Mama from Reverend Milsom's orbit.'

As a non-sequitur, it was masterly. As the carriage jolted over the ruts in the lane, Charles felt his lips twitch and had to struggle to keep his face straight. How did Verity *do* this? 'That seems unnecessarily harsh on the parson,' he said. 'Is there a reason for so callous an act?'

Verity nodded, and now she was not smiling at all. 'Reverend Milsom has pale, fervent eyes, an encroaching disposition and an unrelenting conviction that he is the sole road to salvation. He was most persistent about suggesting private prayer sessions if Mama was finding it a struggle adjusting to widowhood. I happened to mention she only had the use of her pension and this house whilst she remained a widow, since when his visits have become satisfyingly infrequent. I would like to remove her from Kennet End before some gossipy person spreads the word about my uncle's annuity.'

Charles regarded her with exasperation. Not only was there was nothing more likely in a country neighbourhood, it was almost the one circumstance that would reconcile him to their transition to town. 'For someone who claims to hardly stir from the house, you have a profound knowledge of human nature,' he said, sounding huffy even to his own ears.

'Thank you.'

'Are you going to tell me what is it you really want to do in London?'

Verity put her head on one side and studied him, as if weighing him up. It was oddly disconcerting. 'I am going to look for Kitty,' she said.

It was the last thing he had expected. Charles was taken aback, both by the statement and her air of quiet determination. 'Kitty? Your half-sister? Is she missing, then?'

'I do not know. After she eloped

— for which I really cannot blame her, considering how vital and good-humoured Captain Eastwick was, compared to the dry-bones Papa intended marrying her to — Papa refused to have her name mentioned. He didn't make the least push to follow them, and he forbade anyone to read her letters, should she send any. I miss her, Charles. I loved Kitty very much. I want to know where she is. I want to know she is happy.'

Charles wrinkled his brow, trying to recall the facts. 'Captain Eastwick . . . Was he a serving soldier? Suppose he is stationed somewhere distant?'

'I believe he had been injured in Spain and was already invalided out of the army when he came to Newmarket, but if that is not the case, then I can write to her. You will know how to discover the regiment. I think, though, that Kitty is in London.'

'But, Verity, it's been years, surely?'

'Seven. I know it seems unlikely, but when we were at St George's for John and Selina's wedding, I thought I glimpsed her on the pavement amongst the other people. I promise it was not because I was looking for her, because I had no idea she might be there.'

Whatever else Charles's least welcome client was, she was not fanciful. He tried to push away the feeling of foreboding that, for good or ill, he was about to become embroiled in one of Verity's schemes *again*. 'You had better tell me,' he said.

Verity beamed at him. 'You know that there are always people gathered outside a church, out of curiosity or just to see the wedding finery? I was looking around after we came out, because anything was better than the smugness on Selina's face as she accepted congratulations, and I saw Kitty. She was watchful and still, the way I have sometimes seen her, and she had a small girl by the hand. I was *sure* it was her. But she disappeared. I scribbled our direction on a page torn from my pocketbook and tucked it into the palings where she had been standing and I thought perhaps she would contact me, but she never did.'

'The woman you saw was most likely a cut-purse, ready to take her chance with a distracted wedding party. I am afraid I see many such instances during the course of my work.'

She shrugged helplessly. 'Maybe so, but I cannot *not* try, can I? She looked . . . she looked thin.'

Thin. Charles said slowly, 'Have you thought that perhaps the elopement was not everything Kitty had hoped for? Some men, especially if the woman is unhappy at home and supposes herself in love, can be very persuasive.'

'Do you mean she may not be married at all?' Verity bit her lip. 'Then even more must I tell her Papa is dead and she can come back and live with me and Mama. And the child too, if it is hers.'

'Even if, in the eyes of society, she is ruined? That will reflect on you and your mother. Your chances of making a good match would be virtually nil.'

'Charles, she is my *sister*. Mama brought her up as a daughter and still grieves for her loss. How should I care for my reputation if Kitty is in need?'

'John might have something to say on that head.'

'John always has something to say. The dower house is Mama's for as long as she remains unwed. Kitty can live with us until we find somewhere else. And if it effectively disposes of Reverend Milsom's advances, so much the better. Will you help me?'

Charles raised his eyes briefly heavenwards. She already knew he would. Mr Tweedie might depend on him to do the right thing, but Charles never had been able to resist Verity. It was one reason he had not wanted this commission. He sighed. 'We will go to London and I will put you in the way of an investigative agent I have used before. I cannot promise more.'

'Thank you.' She peeped up at him. 'Is this rational behaviour?'

The carriage had turned in at Rooke Hall. Verity's timing was faultless. Charles felt a momentary relief that there was nothing else she could ambush him with. He smiled. 'In my eyes it is.'

*   *   *

'Truly, Jenny, I did feel a little bad teasing Charles when he was so determined to be an upstanding man of business, but it is the right thing to do, and he agreed it in the end. And I very nobly did not remind him that there is nothing he or John can do to *stop* Mama paying a visit to an old friend and taking me with her.'

Jenny Prettyman chuckled. 'Most restrained. Even so, it is as well it was not Mr Tweedie who came to settle your affairs.'

'No indeed. Mama may say Mr Tweedie is a dear sweet man, but I own my heart did leap when I saw Charles descend from the gig, even though *then*

I only had in mind to tax him about Mama's money. I have never not known him amenable and . . . and amiable, even as a boy. Heaven knows he has always come to the rescue when Julia and I found ourselves in a scrape.'

'He is a good man. Adam likes him very much. It cannot have been easy for him to put aside his friends and a life of gentlemanly leisure and work for a living.'

Verity felt a tiny pinprick of shock. Charles was Charles. When the news had been disseminated that he was to follow the law, she had not thought it in any way strange. It had seemed natural that he would want a profession. 'I suppose it could not have been. I had not thought of it before. Women of our class are expected to be biddable and decorative until we marry. If I pull against that, why should not Charles? He is certainly not the type to live without purpose.' *Biddable and decorative*. The two most insipid words in the lexicon. Another thought formulated in her mind. 'Do you like being married, Jenny?'

Her friend laughed. 'Very much. Why do you ask?'

'Because Mama did not, I think. So I was determined never to marry, but you seem quite content. Of course, you have Rooke Hall to manage, and Adam's children and your cousin to look after . . . '

'And our own babe too when spring comes, but that has little to do with the married state. I was never in love before, so I have nothing to compare this with, but my heart lifts when I think of Adam. He is the companion of my life, no matter what other responsibilities we have. My own parents were the same, all in all to each other. Forgive me, but I do not think your mother had a similar affinity with Mr Bowman.'

'No indeed. They were very unalike. It depends on the gentleman, then?'

'The gentleman, what you feel for him, what he feels for you. You will know when it is right.'

Verity nodded. 'I shall remember. Thank you, Jenny. But as my inclination is not to marry if I have enough to live on without doing so, and I go to London solely to search for Kitty, it hardly matters. We are still in mourning for Uncle James, so won't be moving in society, though Julia may have other ideas.'

'Is it your intention to keep Charles with you until you go? Will you both dine here tomorrow and bring your mother? Caroline and Alexander Rothwell are in Newmarket for the whole of October because of the racing. They may be able to join us.'

Verity beamed. 'You are the best of friends. I accept with pleasure. Two days will be perfect as far as our packing is concerned. Anticipating Charles's agreement, I set it in train last night and dispatched a letter from Mama and me to Godmama. He has no option, really, but to escort us. However, your invitation will sweeten the pill and help him justify to himself the delay in returning to his chambers. I believe he knows the Rothwells socially, does he not? He and Alexander and Adam can all talk politics together which will amuse them very well. In truth, Charles could do with a rest from his work. He seems tired, but that may be the result of having his nice tidy plans thwarted. Oh, and I have had another idea. We can ride over to Furze House after we have been to church, so I can show him I am in earnest about removing there. The gardener and his wife are still in their cottage and have a set of keys. I am sure when Charles has seen the rooms and the pleasant prospect, he will agree it is far superior to the dower house, even if it is a trifle shabby.'

'And once you are in London? How will you ensure his cooperation in your quest to search for your sister? He has concerns of his own to deal with. He cannot neglect his other clients.'

'I wouldn't ask him to. If he will but

set me on the right route to finding Kitty, there will be no need for me to disturb him. I have frequently stayed with Julia and her parents before. London is not wholly strange to me.'

Jenny made a wry face. 'It will become more familiar the longer you spend there. From my dealings with Mr Tweedie over the years, much as I esteem the dear man, I cannot say his chambers are very swift to deal even with urgent matters, though events do happen faster now Adam has got into the habit of catching the stage to visit Charles every so often.'

'Well then, I shall take steps to ensure that Charles discovers in himself a compelling need to speed my search.'

★ ★ ★

'I tell you, Adam, if we hadn't been travelling in her own carriage I'd have dumped the minx in the lane and come on alone. It wouldn't surprise me to find all the trunks corded and ready on our return.'

Adam Prettyman laughed and drew them each another tankard. They were in his land office where he found the presence of a barrel of ale made a considerable difference when discussing estate matters with his foreman or the tenant farmers. 'Verity is a determined young woman, but she strikes me as having a good heart.'

'Oh, she has — together with a conviction that she is always right. I hope she will not be too distressed if we do trace her sister. You know as well as I the likely fate of those poor souls who are persuaded to elope to London thinking they are in love.'

Adam's grim expression reflected his own. 'I do indeed. Not only to London. Do you have contacts amongst your more interesting acquaintance who could help if hers is one of those cases?'

His more interesting acquaintance. The Pool, in other words. The loose 'pool of talent' that his one-time school fellow Benedict Fitzgilbert had drawn together to combat the rising tide of lawlessness in London. That was definitely something he would need to hide from Verity.

Fitz had had a simple idea. To recruit gentlemen who had a particular area of expertise, and who shared his own progressive ideas, and to see if they might pool their resources in a war against crime. Fitz provided the funds and the connections, including access to Sir Nathaniel Conant, Chief Magistrate at Bow Street. Charles's contribution was a sound knowledge of the law, a working relationship with London's poor, and a useful affinity with the card table. Other members had other skills.

For the Pool to function successfully, it had to be invisible. Adam was one of the very few people who were privy to Charles's clandestine life. 'Any number,' said Charles, answering him, 'but it will be tricky just now to make contact. The Pool have had whisper of a shadowy gentleman we

51

have suspected the existence of for some time. We think he is behind a number of women's disappearances as well as running a score of unsavoury establishments catering for all degrees of vice. I'm loath to do anything more than tiptoe through the outskirts of his empire until I am more sure of who hides within the rumours.'

'Can you make enquiries for Verity's sister by proxy? Use my name if you wish.'

Charles shook his head. 'Not until we know more. I learned very early not to involve others. This particular shadow has a swift and merciless way with loose mouths. I'll not have retribution falling on the innocent. I've a couple of aliases that will serve if it comes to it. But thank you.'

'It wouldn't be 'involving' me if I made the enquiries myself.'

'I can't do that, Adam.'

'As you wish. It is your fight. But remember, if you need a strong arm, send me word.'

Charles quirked an eyebrow at that. 'Settled life palling on you? Are you hankering for the boards again?'

'Hardly. There is enough to do and more here. I am enjoying the challenge of being a gentleman farmer again, but I'll not deny some action in a good cause wouldn't go amiss. What is the point of being built like a bear and not using it?'

Charles clapped him on the shoulder. 'It's a promise then. If I do track down my shadowy target, there's no one I'd rather have at my back, that's for sure.'

'At your back, is it? I was thinking more side by side. This isn't an idle offer, Charles. I've lost enough actresses and actors to the lures of the city to have no qualms about bringing the puppet masters to justice.'

'Then I will send word if there is time. Meanwhile, shall we join the ladies and see what fresh variation of hell has been cooked up for me?'

'Certainly. I am not sure I envy you this task at least. It is an interesting conundrum, to decide what constitutes rational behaviour. How do you look to resolve it?'

Charles squared his shoulders as if the guillotine, rather than a civilised nuncheon, awaited him in the dining room. 'I don't believe I will have to. By now it has almost certainly been resolved for me.'

4

'I beg your pardon, Hicks.' Charles looked at his man over a forkful of indifferently cooked egg which he was endeavouring to eat with sufficient dispatch that it did not linger overlong in his mouth. 'For a moment, I thought you said a lady had called.'

'I . . . yes, I . . . '

'Good morning, Charles.' Before his appalled eyes, Verity walked past the valet, looking impossibly bright-eyed and alert for a young lady who had endured a lengthy carriage ride the previous day and who had looked set to be talking with his sister far into the night. She removed her gloves as she sat down. 'Pray do not mind me. I did not know at what time you departed for your chambers, so thought it as well to be here early.'

Charles found his voice. 'Do not sit

down. I forbid you to make yourself comfortable. Hicks, procure Miss Bowman a hackney carriage immediately. Are you quite mad, Verity? What are you thinking of, calling on a gentleman at this hour of the morning? Remember your uncle's stipulations on the legacy if nothing else. Ruining both our reputations is *not* rational behaviour.'

'I apologise for putting you out,' replied Verity, not appearing in the least discomposed as she reached forward to test the coffee pot. 'You departed so precipitously yesterday that I had no chance to ask when you would be ready, but I shall know to leave it a further quarter-hour before setting out next time. Do not look so disapproving, it was better that I came inside to wait for you rather than loitering in the street, do you not think?'

'Yes. No. Do not pour that coffee. You are leaving. Verity, do not pour . . . '

'Sit down and finish your egg, Charles, or it will spoil. Do be easy, I am not lost to all reason. I did not come alone. My maid is waiting in the hall.'

'The egg was spoiled before I started it and I have now lost what appetite I once had. I wonder your woman did not refuse to accompany you on such an improper errand.'

'Bridget is the most placid creature in the world. She would not dream of questioning me. Why do you eat food you do not enjoy?'

Charles lowered his voice. 'Because it is a way of giving Hicks extra money for his mother and simpleton sister without offence. Verity, do please think. Do you *want* six months to stretch to nine because of your foolhardiness?'

'Not in the least, which is why I am here rather than listening to Julia's secondhand account of the masquerade her friends attended last week.'

Charles now felt a bolt of terror run through his chest. 'Masquerade?' he said, his voice sharp. 'The one at Vauxhall she was teasing me to take her to? She did not go herself?'

Verity met his eyes. 'She did not, but unless your father and eldest brother modify their relentless criticism of Lieutenant Crisp, there is no saying she might not go another time.'

'Lieutenant Crisp! He may be a lieutenant, but he has no social graces and gives the impression of being an untried puppy. He is the worst possible choice for Julia.'

'Hardly untried if he has seen action. This is unlike you, Charles. You are in general fair-minded. How many times have you met him?'

'My father dislikes the crowd he runs with. Julia needs a strong partner in life, not a weak one.'

'You do not think her capable of discovering this for herself? Opposition without explanation is likely to make her *more* predisposed towards a suitor, rather than less.'

'It is because she is a daughter, not a son. My father was willing enough to let the rest of us make our own mistakes.

You must admit a lady's error is likely to have a more profound effect on her future happiness than a gentleman's is.'

Verity nodded. 'There is truth in that, which is why it is even more important to be told *why* a match is bad.'

'You will see it for yourself when you are in company with the fellow. I cannot think what Julia is about.' He was struck by an idea. 'Turning her thoughts in a better direction *would* be a rational use of your time.'

The room became suddenly icy. 'Poorly done, Charles. Should I find the lieutenant unsuitable, I will naturally share my reservations with Julia for fear of future misery on her part. I do not need your commendation so to do.'

Charles was taken aback at the amount of reproof Verity infused into her tone, the more so because he had known as soon as the words left his mouth that he shouldn't be asking. 'I apologise. That was unworthy on my part.'

She looked at him for a moment.

'Accepted. I will continue to treat Julia in every way as a sister as I always have done, but it is not what I am here for on this occasion, Charles.'

He stood up and held his hand out to her. 'And this is why you should never disturb a man before his first pot of coffee. May we strike a deal, Verity? Will you return to Grosvenor Street, spend the day with Julia and let me make arrangements about other matters? Tomorrow I will conduct you to my chambers to meet with Scrivener, the enquiry agent I mentioned.'

Verity smiled at him and rose to her feet. 'I will. And the scientific lectures?'

'We will call at the Royal Society and I will put your name down for them.'

'Thank you, Charles. You had best finish dressing. Though I do like that robe. It is in every way splendid.'

Charles looked down, startled. He had forgotten he had not yet completed his morning preparations. And now she had seen him in his crimson brocade dressing gown. 'Verity, I . . . '

But she was already walking briskly down the passage. 'Come, Bridget; we are returning to Miss Julia. Ah, Hicks, a hackney to Grosvenor Street by way of Grafton House, if you please.' She raised her voice. 'Mourning gloves, Charles. Nothing frivolous, I promise you.'

Charles watched from the window until he had the evidence of his own eyes that she was being driven away from the Albany, upon which he allowed himself to breathe again. This, he thought, was going to be a very long six months. Which made it all the more puzzling that he should find himself whistling as he abandoned the wreck of his breakfast table and made ready for Middle Temple and his chambers.

* * *

Verity returned to Grosvenor Street much invigorated by a passage of arms with a shopman who claimed to be keeping the last pair of slim-fitting black gloves for another customer and who was thus mistakenly proposing to charge her extra for an instant sale rather than having to wait until the middle of the week for the new stock. So far, the day had proved most satisfactory.

'You look appallingly healthy, Verity. I do hope none of our friends observed you. Did you get your gloves?'

Verity grinned at her friend, arrayed languidly at the breakfast table with both their mamas. 'Good morning, Julia. I did, but in my triumph I forgot black-bordered handkerchiefs so I shall have to go again.' Despite her airy assurances to Charles, Verity knew perfectly well early morning calls to gentlemen weren't the done thing, so had made shopping her excuse for being out betimes. It was safe enough, because she had no expectation that Charles would actually take her to his place of work this morning. Her object had simply been to make it clear she was in earnest about spending time in a rational manner, preferably *before* he heard about the waltz-practice party at the Heywards' this afternoon. She'd hoped he would be so unnerved he would straight away set about finding Kitty and, as it appeared she had been successful, this left the rest of the day to apply herself to her friend's affairs.

'At what time do we go to the Heywards'?' she asked, helping herself to a roll and spreading it with butter. She lowered her voice. 'And will I meet this vexatious new suitor of yours there?'

Julia's eyes twinkled wickedly as she passed the damson preserve. 'Harriet made a point of asking her brother if any of his regiment were free to help us practise,' she murmured. 'At one o'clock,' she said in her normal tones. 'Afterwards, we could call at Hatchards so you can purchase an improving book to impress Charles.'

Mrs Congreve looked up from where she was conversing with Verity's mother. 'Such an odd clause. Was the dear admiral perfectly sound when he stipulated it?'

'We will never know, Godmama. It was added in Newmarket, according to Charles, so possibly he had just had a reverse on a horse. However, it has impelled us to London, which is a very good thing for Mama, and I intend to bother Charles dreadfully with instances of serious behaviour so he will become exhausted long before six months are up and make over Uncle James's estate to me without a murmur. Mama and I can then abandon the dower house and take a *nice* property at the other end of the town from Kennet End.'

'Speaking for myself, I hope Charles will do no such thing,' said Julia.

'Well, you are a poor excuse for a friend. Why, pray?'

'Because as soon as your object is achieved, you will be leaving us for Newmarket again. Life is never tedious when you are here. Do you know how few people I can converse with without becoming bored? One cannot be forever picking apart the gossip and learning new dance steps.'

'Oh, you poor creature. I had no idea all the shops in London had ceased trading,' said Verity sympathetically.

Julia spread her hands. 'With what am I to shop? I am at penury's door until the quarter. Why was I not born as wealthy as Lilith Fitzgilbert? She will also be at the Heywards', incidentally.'

Verity stared in disbelief. 'You are not telling me *Lilith* needs to practise the waltz?'

'Of course not, no more than we do. But she hankers for bosom friends to whom she can unpack her troubles in private. Her aunt has sent them an Italian poet that her stepmother may introduce him into society. The wretched man is presently haunting the house and has fallen madly in love with her.'

'Poor Lilith. I shall be very glad to see her again. I daresay she knows all the galleries where I might improve my mind by viewing important paintings and studying ancient artefacts.'

Julia's lips curved into a smile. 'I have very little doubt of it, and it will enable her to leave the house with impunity. What a happy thought of yours, Verity. We shall become culture hawks together. I foresee a most instructional autumn.'

Julia, thought Verity, was most definitely up to something.

★   ★   ★

As soon as the officers entered Mrs Heyward's saloon in their uniform coats and faultless breeches, Verity predicted which one was Lieutenant Crisp and saw very clearly why Julia's father opposed any sort of match between them. What was not so clear was why Charles had stigmatised him as a puppy. The gentleman in question bowed over Lady Heyward's hand, sent a lazy look at Julia with the merest hint of a smoulder to it, then fell into

66

conversation with the elder Miss Heyward.

Goodness, thought Verity, suddenly very glad she was wearing a high-necked bodice with her pale grey silk. Her friend had certainly caught a lively suitor here.

Engaged in making conversation with the other young ladies and watching the door for Lilith Fitzgerald, she was unaware of Julia's movements until her perfectly modulated voice said, 'Verity, may I present Lieutenant Crisp? Lieutenant Crisp, this is my oldest friend, Miss Bowman. Our cradles were side by side in the nursery.'

Verity gathered her defences and looked up . . . into the disingenuous, freckled face of a very young officer. 'Oh,' she said, taken aback. 'Good afternoon.'

'I am pleased to meet you.' He bent an adoring look on Julia. 'Any friend of Miss Congreve's needs no other recommendation.'

'How absurd you are,' said Julia

indulgently, and from that moment on, Verity knew her friend's family had nothing to fear from Lieutenant Crisp. The other officer, however, who she could see raising a blush on Harriet Heyward's cheek, was different matter entirely.

The Honourable Lilith Fitzgilbert entered the room at that moment and gave a cry of delight at seeing Verity, so she was able to smile in a civil, uncommitted way at Lieutenant Crisp and cross to greet her.

'Lilith, how fortunate. I find myself in great need of your counsel — or more particularly, your blue-stocking tendencies.'

'How lovely to see you, Verity. Pray do speak a little louder. I am not sure all the marriageable gentlemen in the room heard you.'

'Fiddle, none of them are worth wasting the price of a good cultural guide on. I cannot imagine why Julia fills her days with such fribbles. I require knowledge, Lilith.'

Lilith linked her arm in Verity's. 'Now I know you are back in town. How may I help? More to the point, why?'

'The most tiresome thing. I have to prove to Charles that I am spending six months in a rational manner before I can gain access to my uncle's legacy and take a nicer house for Mama. We have seen the very one and I am now in a fever lest someone else finds it. It is a little shabby to be sure, but that means it is a bargain. Even Charles reluctantly admits it to be a good investment, if rather too large. I need to draw up a programme of cultural recreation to impress him with my seriousness, and then I am sure Furze House is as good as mine.'

'That is easily done. There are small galleries everywhere. Somerset House will provide you with easily a month of study taken by itself. Do you wish for just the programme to be set out, or is it your intention to actually visit the exhibits?'

'She wishes to visit them, naturally,' answered Julia, gliding towards them and taking Lilith's other arm. 'You and I shall go with her to witness Charles's proof.' Her gaze rested briefly on the cluster of red coats by the piano, where the Heywards' governess was preparing to strike up a waltz. 'It will be a beautifully unexceptional way to spend several afternoons. I daresay the novelty of it will easily attract us an escort, should we wish for one.'

Verity and Lilith exchanged glances. 'Julia dearest,' said Verity, 'I have the strongest suspicion that mine is not the only ulterior motive here. Are you going to enlighten me?'

Julia sent her a provocative look. 'Now where would be the amusement in that?'

5

Charles Congreve, that evening, was present at a select dinner given by Benedict Fitzgilbert. So select, in fact, that they waited on themselves from the array of dishes on the table.

'No Rothwell tonight, Fitz?' asked Nicholas Dacre, lazily filling his glass before passing the bottle on.

'He is not in town until next week,' answered their host. 'Caroline has horses running at Newmarket.'

Nick's face darkened. 'Which is where I should be if I hadn't had to dance attendance on my grandfather.'

'My condolences. How is he?'

'Likely to live for the next twenty years despite what he and his doctors predict. I swear the old man plans these deathbed scenes for just when it is most inconvenient to his warring descendants. I might get off to Newmarket early tomorrow if only to get the family poison out of my system. I'll still get some racing, even if it is too late for the certainty I had for today.'

'Your tips are always certainties,' said Charles. 'You should wager on Caroline's horses. I was at dinner with them a few days ago in Newmarket. Solange is in foal and Caro claims Rufus is running better than ever on the strength of it. Alex, by the way, asked me to pass on that he is now established in the reform movement and anti-slavery camp in the House and is doing his best to press for changes.'

Dacre's eyes widened. 'That must have been an interesting dinner. No one suspected you and Rothwell to be more than casual acquaintances?'

'My dear Nick, the ladies are all close friends. We could have referred to the Pool out loud and they would not have remarked it. They were talking so hard about Verity Bowman's inheritance and how taking Furze House would provide incontrovertible proof of spending the next six months in a rational manner due to the necessity of turning it into a habitable residence, that it was impossible to introduce another topic of conversation at all. In the course of a single dinner, they had gutted the place, knocked three or four rooms together, furnished and decorated it, modernised the kitchen, let out the back premises to make the place pay and planned their first party.'

His companions roared with laughter. 'It sounds ideal,' said Dacre. 'Why do you not let Miss Bowman have her head? Is the house bad? Where is it?'

'Towards the heath on the Suffolk side. The house is far too large, but it is sound,' said Charles shortly. 'Which is more than I can say for Verity. If I did as you suggested, she would be gulled on all sides by tradesmen and have spent her legacy by Christmas. Probably on some good cause totally unrelated to the house.'

'Surely she cannot be that hen-witted?'

Charles looked at him with a bitter expression. 'She is not in the least hen-witted. She merely views the world from a different perspective. For example, I'll take long odds you never had to break *your* sister and her madcap friend back *into* school because they had decided you needed your spirits lifting before your *viva* and had not troubled themselves to get permission for an *exeat.*'

'No,' said Nicholas, a little stunned. 'No, I can't say I did.'

'Precisely. To return to what we were talking about, Fitz, I have an offer from Adam Prettyman. He is at our service if we are ever, as he put it, in need of a gentleman as big as a bear with a gift for mimicry and a hard-won knowledge of rough fighting. As you know, I had dealings with him during that shocking business with the Earl of Harwood. I have got to know him pretty well and thought for some time he would be a useful addition to the Pool.'

Fitzgilbert nodded. 'Noted. And as

his attorney you have an unexceptional reason for meeting him. Yes then, you'll let him know? Good. To business, gentlemen. I have had a communication from Sir Nathaniel Conant. The man found in the Thames last week has been identified as one of Nash's builders. Nash reported to Sir Nathaniel a while ago he'd received threats that if he didn't pay a certain sum of money, building work on his New Street would be disrupted. Our shadow-man appears to be expanding his areas of interest. Thoughts?'

Charles put Verity firmly to the back of his mind and concentrated on the far easier problem of how to unmask an unknown extortionist who had all of London to hide in.

*   *   *

Verity was ready in good time for her day with Charles. She was confident she'd said enough about Furze House for the idea to be fixed. She did not wish him to become so aggravated that he fulfilled one wish without also making a push on finding Kitty. During breakfast, her mother very nearly scuppered the plan by wondering aloud whether this might not be an ideal time to call on Mr Tweedie herself regarding her annuity, but Verity, with great presence of mind, reminded her of Mr Tweedie being much engaged at present and put forward the counter suggestion that it would be far more pleasant to extend him an invitation to call at Grosvenor Street at his own convenience. They would then be warm and comfortable, unconstrained for time and while they discussed financial matters they could have refreshments far superior to any provided at his chambers.

The idea found favour, her mother wrote a note for Mr Tweedie, and Verity waited, outwardly calm, for Charles to collect her and take her away from curious ears. It was not precisely that she didn't want anyone else privy to her quest, it was more that she didn't want her mother to build up her hopes and then be disappointed if she failed. She also didn't want anyone putting well-meaning obstacles in her way.

Charles arrived in a hackney carriage looking in every way smart and sober. 'You look very well,' she said, subjecting him to a friendly scrutiny, 'though I cannot help regretting the loss of that crimson robe.'

'I fear not all my clients have your discernment,' he said gravely. 'One day, perhaps, I may lead a revolution in exciting attire for the legal profession. Until then I had best follow the flock if I am to eat and pay the rent on my rooms.'

Good. He was in an agreeable mood. Verity smiled sunnily at him and kept up a bright flow of conversation on the way to his chambers, remarking on the shop fronts in Bond Street, the entrance to his Albany buildings and the imposing appearance of Somerset

House, which she hadn't realised was so large and handsome.

'We will see more of it later,' said Charles. 'The Royal Academy, Royal Society and Society of Antiquities are all based there, as well as various exhibitions. For now, Mr Scrivener will be waiting for us.'

The hackney stopped at Temple Bar, where they alighted, Verity taking Charles's arm as they walked though the archway to the buildings of the Middle Temple.

'Oh, but these are charming!' she exclaimed, looking around. 'I have never been in this part of London before.'

Charles slowed, matching his pace to hers. 'There was no reason for you to have done. This is a place of profession-als. In my first days here I felt very much as if I was attending an over-large house party given by someone I was not familiar with. Everyone appeared to know each other and there was a mysterious code of conduct to learn before I was accepted.'

'Poor Charles. And do you now know where to assemble for dinner and which boot boy to bribe to get the best shine on your footwear?'

He laughed. 'Something of the sort. Down this way and around the corner. The buildings are interesting rather than handsome. Not all chambers reflect their external architecture. Mr Tweedie's set of rooms are a good size, in some of the others I am amazed the clerks can find anything at all. The legal profession uses a great deal of paper, and all of it has to be stored.'

'Mama wishes to invite Mr Tweedie to call on her when it is convenient. I have a letter from her. She was sorry he could not come into Newmarket himself after Uncle James's death, though I personally was very well pleased it was you. She told me she remembered Mr Tweedie as having been very unobtrusive and kind during the preparations for her wedding to Papa, and she still feels grateful for it, even after twenty years.'

Charles grinned. 'Do not tell him I said so, but he can be kind indeed. He was very patient with me when I was still learning my way around the various articles and clauses. I am sure he will be happy to call on Mrs Bowman. She seemed to have made quite an impression on him in former times. He told me she was the prettiest, liveliest young lady in Suffolk twenty years ago.'

Verity stopped in genuine astonishment. 'Goodness. Did he really say that? I love her dearly, but I would never have described her as lively. And yet, I do not know . . . I remember when she used to tell us stories of gods and myths and so forth, the tales would come alive.' *Pretty and lively. Who would have thought it?* 'If that is the effect marriage and children have,' she continued, 'I am more than ever determined to remain single.'

A conscience-stricken expression crossed Charles's face. 'I should not have said anything. You will ruin my professional reputation, Verity. You lull me into talking indiscreetly as if we were friends, not attorney and client.'

She gave a peal of laughter and tucked her hand into his arm again. 'How foolish you are, Charles. How should we not be friends? It is by far the most comfortable way of going on.'

★   ★   ★

Lord above, how did she do this? In general, he had no difficulty becoming Mr Congreve, attorney-at-law, during the day and Charles, youngest son of Anthony Congreve Esquire, whenever he was required for a family party. The rare occasions with friends when he was simply Charles were as jealously guarded as the railed gardens of London's squares, but Verity seemed able to pick the locks simply by laying her hand upon the gate.

'You are dangerous, Verity,' he said, steering her with no little effort towards his building when she would have strayed to observe the water jets in Fountains Court. 'Perhaps I should approve Furze House and pack you off back to Newmarket immediately, before you compromise my working life any further.'

'Thank you, Charles. As soon as I have found Kitty, I will go with pleasure. I will send you regular reports on the progress of the work so if my grandmother and uncle ever dispute the bequest, you will have proof of how diligent I am being.'

Which meant, he realised with disbelief as he got her indoors and ascending to the clerks' room, that he had agreed once again to one of her suggestions. She was impossible. How could a professional clause-wrangler like himself give in without argument so easily, and on so little evidence of a successful outcome?

Though it would be successful, he admitted grudgingly, because everything Verity turned her attention to enjoyed some measure of success. The key question lay in determining the price for that success.

Mr Scrivener was waiting. He followed them into Charles's office and sat, pencil in hand, ready for instructions.

'Eastwick, Captain,' he murmured. '1810 or thereabouts. Catherine Margaret Bowman, known as Kitty. Brown hair, grey eyes, slight frame. I will call next week to report progress. Usual terms, Mr Congreve?'

'Certainly, Mr Scrivener. Make the accounts to my office, if you please.'

Charles saw the man out and returned to find Verity looking a little blank.

She met his eyes ruefully. 'A week? I had hoped it would be sooner.'

'It may be. We cannot tell at this stage. Come, we will put your name down for the Royal Society lectures, and then I will escort you to Grosvenor Street.'

'Oh, but I am to stay with you the whole day, am I not? The others will have driven out by now.'

Charles felt a rush of exasperation, mixed with just a tinge of uncertainty as to what he had promised her yesterday. 'Verity, I have work to do. I have to go to Bow Street to meet a client.'

'Is that the magistrate's court? I have never been there. It sounds as if it would be a rational place to visit.'

'Rational possibly, but it is not a place for a lady. I will be at least an hour inside.'

'I may watch the proceedings, may I not?'

Charles's patience snapped. Perhaps the shock of observing the sessions would convince her of the absurdity of going about with him during working hours. 'You may. Very well, but on your own head be it.'

He gathered the papers he would need and swept her out. Striding up Middle Lane, he felt her hand creep under his arm.

'I fear I am being a great trial to you, Charles,' she said in a small voice.

Her head was downbent, her bonnet

shaded her face. He slowed his pace and laid his hand over hers, already ashamed of his show of temper. 'It is your uncle I am wishing to damnation, not you,' he said, not entirely accurately. 'I beg pardon for my incivility. We will have a rational morning, Verity, and perhaps one or two more, but it cannot be *every day*.'

'No, I see that. You need not worry. I will go with Julia and Lilith to the exhibitions at other times. Lilith knows a great many sensible, improving places for me to visit.'

Charles stopped. 'Lilith Fitzgilbert?' he asked.

Verity looked up at him enquiringly. 'Yes. Do you know her?'

'I have been introduced. It is an unusual name. She impressed me as being a very well-educated young lady.' He started walking again, one part of his mind wondering if Verity going about with Fitz's sister would make things awkward for them, or whether they could turn it to account.

6

Curious, thought Verity. Something had stopped Charles mid-stride, and that was not a thing that often happened. Something about Lilith. She tucked the circumstance away and instead looked around her with curiosity as they walked. There was a good deal of busyness about this part of London, with gentlemen of many professions hurrying to and fro as well as the street children who seemed to be everywhere.

In Bow Street itself, Charles had a word with the impressive personage behind the desk, then returned to her.

'I have to go to the cells to talk to my gentleman. The sessions are in progress, so you must wait for a break before you can enter. I do not like to leave you without an escort, but if you sit on this bench where you are in sight of the clerk, you will be quite safe. Another time, we must bring your maid or a footman with us. I will be as quick as I can.'

'Dear Charles, I think we are both learning today. Do not hurry back if haste means you cannot help your client properly. I shall be most prudent, I assure you.'

'That,' said Charles, 'would be a miracle I am not sure I deserve.'

He disappeared though a passage leading to the rear of the building. Verity chuckled, exchanged a smile with the clerk at the desk and prepared to be amused. An enormous variety of people seemed to proceed through the entrance hall, some blustery with importance, some timid, some loud and some simply weary.

Verity watched as a skinny clerk was brought in by his employer and charged with fraud. Several urchins were dragged through the door having been cried as thieves, a stout, painted matron with a great many bracelets was accused of running a brothel and a very elegant gentleman supervised the deposit of a couple of ruffians, both of whom had their hands efficiently tied and were in the care of the gentleman's groom. All the charges were written down and the parties directed to either a waiting area or the cells. All apart from the elegant gentleman who got a respectful murmur of 'Thank you, Sir Philip,' and an assurance that a messenger would be sent when it was his turn to give evidence.

The next gentleman to march up to the desk was one Verity took an instant dislike to. He strode in pulling a comely woman by her wrist.

'Theft,' he said in a loud, important voice. 'I've come to report outright theft.'

The woman twisted out of his grasp and plumped herself down on the bench next to Verity. 'It is not theft,' she called forcefully, rubbing her wrist. 'I'll sit here while you say your piece, then I'll stand up like a Christian and say mine.'

'Are you quite well?' asked Verity with concern. 'Your wrist seems very sore.'

'It's been better, that's for sure.' The woman adjusted a shawl which wasn't doing much to cover her generous decolletage, and glanced at her in a frank, friendly fashion. 'Here to watch the proceedings? I've done that in my time. Near as good as the theatre without the shilling you pay on the door. Not so many laughs though. Molly Turner's my name.'

Verity shook the proffered hand. 'Verity Bowman. Why has that gentleman brought you here?'

Molly snorted. 'He's no gentleman. He stops me in the street and offers me a shilling to eat with him. Said he likes to have company. Well, some of them are like that and who am I to turn down a free meal? So we eat, he puts a shilling on table, I picks it up, he cries thief.'

'That's despicable,' said Verity, feeling her eyes grow wide.

'True as I'm sitting here, and so I shall tell the magistrate. He then says if I'm nice to him, he won't press charges. Nice. Ha, I know what that means. His sort like the power, see? Well, I'm not having that. Not that I'm above it, you understand, but as a proper business transaction, not a threat, and for more'n a shilling too. Oh, I could jump in the river for being so taken in. Now I have to defend myself against theft.'

'Will the judge believe you?'

'Pray he does. If I'm sent for trial and convicted, it's transportation.' She gave a harsh laugh. 'And if I'm acquitted, I'll no doubt face a charge of prostitution and then I'm for the Bridewell. What will Ma and the kiddies do then? Pity I don't talk nice like you. Then the magistrate would know I was respectable.'

Verity's sense of justice was stung. She gave Molly a candid inspection. Her clothes were not propitious, but . . . 'Could you sit more upright? I have noticed that the straighter one's back, the less people are inclined to believe you may be plotting mischief. And — oh, I know — I cannot give you my pelisse for respectability, but if you can shield me for a moment . . . '

Molly obligingly angled her body, saying, 'Here, miss, you've a smut on your brow. Let me wipe it off for you.'

'Splendid,' said Verity breathlessly, having wrestled her lawn fichu off inside her clothing. 'Now, tuck this around your neck inside your bodice, pull the ribbon around your neckline tighter, and wear your shawl higher on your shoulders. There. I hope it helps.'

'You're a treasure and no mistake.' Molly swiftly effected the transformation, then went to the desk to give her version of events while an official escorted Verity to a bench inside the courthouse to watch the cases.

The proceedings were fast and perplexing, the magistrate seeming to listen to the charge, absorb the statements and decide whether to send the accused person for trial almost in the same breath. Verity's head was spinning by the time Molly and her accuser were brought in.

A flicker of recognition crossed the magistrate's features. After listening to the gentleman repeating his confident charge of theft, he said, 'You seem sadly unlucky in your choice of eating companions. I believe this to be the third time in five weeks you have brought a similar charge. Mrs Turner is plainly a respectable woman. The case is dismissed.'

Verity smiled with relief and was startled when Charles tapped her on the shoulder.

'Have you seen enough? Are you ready to leave now?'

'Yes, but it is bewildering. You must explain it properly to me. What does commit for trial mean?'

'That the victim and the accused must repeat the charge and the defence in front of judge and jury at the Old Bailey. They may also call witnesses to their character, or to the theft or whatever crime the victim claims has been committed.'

'I see. How does the magistrate decide so fast what to do?'

'He has many years experience. Certain crimes are considered minor, such as breaking the peace, others are more serious and must go for trial. Theft, murder, fraud, treason, arson . . . There are many more.'

They had reached the door and were descending the steps to the street, when a boy ran up to Charles and pulled on his sleeve.

'Thomas? What is it?'

'It's Pa.'

Charles muttered under his breath. 'Already? Where and when?'

'Old Bailey, sir. Now.'

Charles cursed and looked down the street to wave energetically at a hackney carriage. 'Find Jenkins and bring him, if you can. I beg your pardon, Verity, but your education is about to take a further turn. To the Old Bailey, if you please.'

Verity found herself bundled in without ceremony. The boy had disappeared, but she saw a pair of heels vanish in the throng and a slight figure weave towards an alleyway. 'Charles?'

Charles was staring out of the grimy window. He looked back at her, troubled but decisive. 'I could wish you in Grosvenor Street, but as you are not I must tell you certain things which, while they are not in any way secret, I would prefer not to be the subject of drawing room discussion.'

Verity nodded.

'Very well. I do not always deal with settlements and wills and land contracts. There are many people who through lack of education, or illiteracy, or feeble-mindedness are accused, or taken up by the authorities, and are not able to fashion themselves a defence. Some of these people I try to help by ascertaining facts that the accuser — the supposed victim — has suppressed. Thomas is the son of a coal merchant who has been accused of theft by one of his customers. The customer says he paid for coal, but only half of it was delivered. The coal merchant knows he delivered the whole order. I found a groom who saw the delivery, saw it inspected, saw the coalman paid, saw him drive away. I have taken a statement from the groom, but the man himself would lend more weight.'

Questions rose to Verity's lips, but they had arrived at the Old Bailey and she was being hurried inside. Charles had a word with a gentleman in a brown coat and they passed through into some sort of gallery.

To Verity's swimming senses, the proceedings seemed to take very little more time than they had in the Bow Street courthouse. Charles was so intent on the scene that she didn't like to disturb him, so it was a few minutes before she could sort out who was speaking and what their function was.

There was a flurry of movement, everyone seemed to breathe and the noise level rose, then a clerk was banging with some sort of hammer and a charge was read out.

Verity heard the words ' . . . *wilfully stealing a handkerchief from . . .* ' and then lost the rest. A stout man repeated the charge, pointed over to a bench, another man nodded and agreed that he'd witnessed the theft. There were more voices, then a juryman said 'Guilty' and the judge perfunctorily pronounced the accused to be sentenced to death.

Verity felt a shocked jolt run through her, even more so when a small girl was led away, her face white and pinched. She turned to Charles, appalled. 'I cannot believe it. That child is to die for stealing a handkerchief? *A handkerchief?*'

Charles's face twisted. 'I knew I should not have brought you here. I am every kind of fool and I apologize profoundly. Verity, theft of all property worth a shilling or more attracts the death sentence, but it is rarely carried out. The cost of the handkerchief will be valued at less than a shilling and the sentence commuted.'

Verity's distress eased a little. 'Oh. Oh, well that is better. Commuted to what?'

Charles hesitated, looking wretched. 'Transportation. Hard labour. But very often the accused are not taken to the ships at all.'

Transportation. Away from family and friends and everything they have known. Verity swallowed. 'But some are? Why do they steal when the consequences are so final?'

'For food. For clothing. In the country, a family may scratch enough food for themselves from the soil. Here in the city it must be bought. A penny from a stolen handkerchief goes frighteningly far in a desperate household.'

'Can nothing be done?'

'Who is to do it? It is impossible to employ all the poor people in London. Hush, this is my man. I must be ready to go down.'

Verity had never felt so cold. She sat in a frozen numbness through the charge and the depositions. She watched as Charles handed in the statement and was glad when the jury found the coal merchant not guilty. She stirred only when Charles reappeared beside her and put his hand on her arm.

'Come, I will take you home,' he said in a gentle voice.

She managed to wait until they were out in the hallway before she turned blindly to him and hid her face in his coat.

His arms were comfortable around her, strong and firm. 'I know,' he murmured. 'This is why I do what I can.'

*　　*　　*

Fool. Imbecile. Idiot. Charles castigated himself over and over as he summoned a hackney carriage and helped Verity inside. He should never

98

have taken her to the Old Bailey sessions. A sheltered country upbringing was no preparation for the desperate wave of humanity to be found in the cells, waiting their turn for justice, if justice could ever be found in an unequal society.

She sat close to him in the carriage, but quiet, leaving him to wrestle with a second problem. He needed to get a message urgently to Fitz. The man he had seen at Bow Street had let slip information that a slave trader was in London from Liverpool, and was looking for investors. Slave trading was illegal. If they could obtain evidence against the man leading to a successful prosecution, that would be one more foul outlet shut down.

Alex Rothwell moved in the right circles but he was well known as an abolitionist and a reformer, so would never be accepted by the trader. Fitz, on the other hand, had money and position. The rogue merchant would believe him out of sheer greed. The question was how to get word to him without suspicion. As a rule the members of the Pool kept as far apart as possible. Slave trading was nothing to do with their current investigations, but as they suspected the shadow master they were after was someone high up, Fitz especially had to stay clear of the rest of them. Charles was loathe to use a street boy to carry a note that could be easily discovered and both ends then traced to make a connection. The same went for a public messenger.

Verity stirred. 'I beg your pardon for being such poor company. I will not be so overset another time. I am glad you help these people, Charles.'

He felt an unexpected glow at her praise. 'It is little enough I do, but it is a start.'

'I see now why you are always working. What do you do this evening? Julia and I are going to a soiree at Lady Fitzgilbert's house. The music will be indifferent, but our main purpose is to support Lilith in the face of her stepmama's guests and discuss a programme of rational occupation for me.' She gave a small, unhappy laugh. 'I hardly feel I need it after today. That child's face. I cannot believe I will ever be frivolous again.'

Charles straightened up so fast his head hit the roof of the carriage. *Lady Fitzgilbert*. See where virtue got you. He could hardly believe his good fortune. Even if Fitz was not at home, he could ask a footman to take a note to his study. 'I agree, it is difficult to be cheerful in the face of the misery at the Old Bailey, but I would be sad never to hear you laugh again. Does my mother go tonight, or shall I accompany you and Julia? Would that please you?'

She looked at him, astonishment writ so plain on her face that he felt a twinge of guilt at dissembling. 'Very much, but it will please Godmama more. She says she has given up on you visiting with the fashionable set in the evenings. I do not think she quite understands the value of an income and how much more pleasant it is to have money than not to have it, nor how hard you work to achieve an equable state.'

He laughed, amused. 'Finances have never been my mother's strong suit. At what time is the soiree?'

'I do not know. Timing means very little to Julia. You had best dine in Grosvenor Street. Charles, you do understand the soiree is being given by Lady Fitzgilbert? An ear for music is not generally counted amongst the most plentiful of her gifts.'

'I feel I should make amends to you for taking you to the Old Bailey this afternoon.'

'Fudge. You have another purpose in mind. Oh, how silly of me. I should advise you it is by no means certain Lieutenant Crisp will be present.'

Charles sat back, content to leave that idea in Verity's head. 'I will endeavour to bear the disappointment.'

7

'Charles is to accompany us? You cannot have explained the evening to him properly.'

Verity was curled up on her friend's bed, watching her complete her toilette. She did not see how anyone could stigmatise Julia as bubble-headed when her attention to the details of her costume was so devastatingly accurate. She must have nestled the pearl sprig amongst her blonde curls quite half a dozen times until she was satisfied.

'I did explain. I even warned him about the music. Julia, you are so beautiful. Why are you still unwed and not queening it as London's top political hostess?'

'No title. Small dowry. Nobody has asked me. Also, there is my slight handicap . . . '

'Which you nevertheless manage to

hide from the polite world.'

'With the help of my friends.' She blew Verity a kiss in the mirror. 'This is really very unlike Charles. I am quite intrigued. Did you also tell him of Lilith's aunt's Italian poet?'

'I may have neglected to mention that. Have you thought Charles might be escorting us in order to observe Lieutenant Crisp?'

'That would be underhand indeed,' said Julia. But she spoke absently, paying more attention to the precise size of her satin bow and the fall of her pale pink gauze overdress than to the prospect of her brother rending her swain limb from limb during the evening's recital.

Verity noted her unconcern, more than ever convinced that her friend had another scheme in train entirely. 'Who else will we meet tonight?'

'Everyone who is not going to the Athertons' party or the Silverwood ball. You will be able to tell the ones who did not receive cards for either. They will wear a simpering expression and say there is something so uplifting about listening to music in quiet appreciation, rather than shouting to make yourself heard over the crush in the refreshment room. That is the ladies. The gentlemen will play cards wherever they are.'

'Lady Fitzgilbert is not so eccentric as to ban the card room? That will please Charles.'

'Heavens, no. She'd never attract anyone. Besides, Benedict wouldn't let her. It is his house since his father died and though Lady Fitz may think she orders things, it is Benedict and Lilith who see to it. Lilith says it is bearable when it is only her stepmother inviting starving artists to dinner, but when her aunt sends dreadful proteges to London for the family to promote, it is the outside of enough.'

Verity frowned. 'The proteges do not live in the house?'

'Benedict is a baron now. There are limits. But they call on Lady Fitz and frequently neglect to leave. And with her and Lilith's aunt being bosom friends . . . '

'Goodness, I thought I had problems with Reverend Milsom laying siege to Mama. No wonder Lilith was looking oppressed. It explains why she was so eager to join my rational-behaviour programme.'

Julia took one last critical look in the glass. 'I advised her to direct the poet to the kitchens so he can scour dishes in exchange for his keep. I doubt she will though. For someone so inquiring and studious, she is ridiculously conventional. Hey ho, let us go down to dinner and see whether Charles has thought better of his offer. I wonder if he thinks to look for a rich wife and that is why he is escorting us?'

'Charles wishes to marry?'

'He hasn't said so, but why else would he put up with poor music and bad poetry? I do not think he earns a great deal as an attorney though he is always well turned out. Heavens, Verity, have you looked at yourself since you dressed? Sometimes I despair of you.'

Verity scrambled off the bed and submitted to having her hair ornament reset and her gown pulled straight. The idea that Julia might be right about Charles made her uneasy. She hadn't forgotten his start when she'd mentioned Lilith's name, and Lilith would be quite a catch in a financial sense. But fortune hunting did not accord with the intent, caring man she had seen with her own eyes today, even if it would give him more of an income to expend on helping the poor.

⋆   ⋆   ⋆

Lady Fitzgilbert's soirees were a byword for informality, said Julia as the carriage bore them towards Bedford Square. This, reflected Verity after they had been there for half an hour, was something of an understatement. A quantity of spindly gilded chairs had been scattered in artistic groups about the well-lit, cream-panelled room. People stood or sat as they pleased, being served lemonade, ratafia and what Verity guessed from Charles's face to be an indifferent wine.

'Julia tells me the cook is very good,' she teased, after he had made a perambulation of the room and failed to find anything better.

'I look forward to it,' replied Charles. 'Assuming we are allowed to eat without being given indigestion.'

Verity made a face. He had a point. Lady Fitzgilbert's creative muse seemed to function by causing her to clap her hands at erratic intervals and announce a performer plucked from the circulating hopefuls. Invariably this occurred just when Verity had succeeded in starting a conversation. Leaving off discussions in order to listen to the entertainment made for a very disjointed evening.

To her surprise, Charles had not disappeared into the card room at the first warble of the flute, nor at the muddled, powerful lament that followed. Nor, from what she had seen of his movements (not that she had been watching, naturally) did he seem to be seeking out well-dowered ladies or paying particular attention to Lilith. She was about to reward this good behaviour by confiding another tip from Julia when Lady Fitzgilbert clapped her hands again.

Charles listened to the new musician for a full ten seconds before turning to Verity. 'What is this appalling noise?'

'Hush. He is a violinist, Charles.'

'Are you sure? Has your friend checked that the kitchen still has its full complement of cats?'

Verity bit her lips together. 'You heard Lady Fitzgilbert's introduction. The poor man fled from Napoleon to be here tonight.'

'I had not realised the emperor was so much of a music lover. Nor that it commonly takes two years to cross the channel.'

Verity directed a hasty, apologetic

smile at the scandalised ladies nearby and drew Charles to a row of chairs at the side of the room out of earshot.

'These are the most hideously uncomfortable chairs I have ever had the misfortune to sit on,' he grumbled.

'That is hardly my problem. I did warn you, Charles. Why did you come with us when you knew what it would be like?'

'The motive escapes me. The music is bad enough, but was there some reason why you did not also warn me about the poet?'

'Oh dear. Were you introduced? As I understand it, Lilith's late father's sister collects exigent artists abroad and sends them to Lady Fitzgilbert in order that London society may marvel at their genius. This has not turned out to be a very rational evening, has it? Would it help if I passed on the information that Lilith's brother keeps a very good cellar for the more discerning visitor, quite separate from the refreshment served to his stepmother's soiree guests? Julia says you simply murmur *Lord Fitzgilbert's claret* to the footman and the proceedings will take on a far rosier hue.'

Charles looked at her in amazement. 'How did she discover that? I cannot believe her ineffectual lieutenant is one of Lord Fitzgilbert's close circle. I see he and his friends have escaped the barracks again to be with us tonight.'

'Don't be unkind. Julia always knows everything. It comes of being interested in people. She watches and listens and has an excellent memory. Also Lilith is our friend.'

'Even so, I should not presume on Lord Fitzgilbert's hospitality until I have received permission.'

'Then go and ask him! See, he has just entered by the far door. I shall listen to the music for both of us.' Verity fixed a soulful expression on her face and let her gaze wander the room. She saw Charles and their host shake hands. Good. Now he would be less acerbic about the company, though she secretly rather enjoyed the turn his wit took when he was disgruntled. Dear Charles, it was very good of him to have stayed in the main room so long. She was still watching him fondly when she saw Lord Fitzgilbert pocket a folded note that Charles appeared to have slipped him.

She stiffened, outraged. *That* was why Charles had accompanied them tonight. He had some sort of covert understanding with Lilith's brother whilst pretending all along that they were barely acquainted. It took her a moment to recognise the emotion that beset her as chagrin.

The violin stopped wailing, much to her relief. Verity blinked to clear her vision and focused on Julia at the centre of a laughing group, having her hand kissed, presumably in response to some pleasantry she had made about the music. Her admirer was the officer who had given her that long look at the waltz practice. Julia withdrew her hand

and let it flutter chastely over her bodice.

Verity's eyes sharpened for a second moment of disbelief. Unless she was very much mistaken, a scrap of paper had been tucked inside the neckline as Julia's fingers had rested there. Was everybody in this salon passing notes to each other? She stood abruptly and was taken by surprise when Charles appeared back at her elbow.

'You were right,' he said, toasting her with a glass of deep ruby wine. 'We must thank Julia.'

'Charles, are you *using* me?' demanded Verity, too jolted to be subtle.

He did not pretend to misunderstand. 'Ah. Only as much as you are using me. I apologise. I must be losing my touch. Did anyone else notice?'

'I do not believe so. It was not you who gave it away. I saw Lilith's brother hide the note.'

'How clumsy of Fitz. I must tell him you rumbled us. That will hurt his pride. Verity, I have no right to ask, but

113

could you perhaps forget anything you might have seen in that corner of the room?'

She was even more hurt by this request than by the original deception. 'You have no *need* to ask it of me either. I will forget until it suits me to remember.'

'I beg your pardon. I should have known. May we discuss programmes of rational study with your friend before we leave?'

Verity glanced across the room to where Julia and her mysterious suitor were now talking to other people. 'I think that would be a very good idea.'

Just then, Lady Fitzgilbert gave another of her sharp claps.

'Oh dear,' said Verity. 'I am very much afraid we must wait until after the poet has had his turn.'

Charles grasped her elbow. 'Not on any account. I have listened to his utterings for ten full minutes already.' He towed her masterfully across the room. 'Miss Fitzgilbert, I wonder if I might trouble you for a morsel of food for Miss Bowman. She has been overcome by the quality of the performances tonight and requires a quiet seat and some sustenance, the better to reflect on them.'

'Charles, you are completely shameless,' said Verity, once the supper room was attained.

'But wonderfully enterprising,' added Lilith, looking at Charles with approval, 'I can now be solicitous towards Verity and not have to look interested in that wretched Italian's outpourings. I suppose it is too much to hope that you will come to all our soirees this season, Mr Congreve?'

Verity opened her mouth to say something caustic about only if Charles wanted to contact Lord Fitzgilbert, but closed her lips in time, wondering at herself both for the near-loss of discretion and for the idiotic way the circumstance rankled. Charles's regretfully evasive reply answered the tone of the exchange far better.

She took refuge in a glass of lemonade and a selection of patties from the refreshment table. At least Charles did not seem to be making a play for her friend, she thought, then stopped, appalled at herself. Charles would make an excellent husband for any lady. She should be encouraging him if he liked Lilith. Was she was still out of sorts from this morning? Surely she was not such a poor creature? With an assumption of enthusiasm she gave her full attention to her friends and enquired about the Somerset House exhibitions.

★ ★ ★

'So this is where you are,' said Julia, dropping down into the chair next to Verity as the doors opened on a wave of people coming through from the other room. 'Glorious voice, your poet,' she added to Lilith, 'but substance sadly lacking, I feel. Not that I am an expert in the Italian tongue.'

'You spent a deal of time talking to him, Miss Congreve.' The lazy observation was made by the older lieutenant. It was clear he was the leader amongst Julia's escort of officers.

'I was *listening* to him, Lieutenant Neville. There is a difference. Now, who will fetch me a . . . oh, thank you, Lieutenant Crisp, how very thoughtful. I declare I am quite parched. Are you as quick with all your military duties?'

Verity listened affectionately as her friend teased the young men. Even in this company, she had a light address and a way of drawing people in that made the occasion sparkle.

Charles did not appear so impressed. 'Are you still overset, Miss Bowman? Would you rather we took our departure as soon as my sister is ready?' His tone was so attentive that Verity would have been touched were not for the fact that she had not felt unwell in the first place and her role here was clearly to opt for a swift exit.

'Oh, pray do not leave so early,' said

Lilith. 'I'm sure Verity is much recovered. Here is my brother come to join us. Benedict, you know Mr Congreve, I feel sure. Will you take him off to the card room as a reward for bearing with the proceedings so far and play a rubber or two of piquet together? I am depending on Julia to hasten everybody away at the end of the evening. She does it with a far more natural air than I ever manage.'

Lieutenant Crisp cleared his throat. 'If Miss Bowman wishes to leave early, I should be very happy to be honoured with the privilege of escorting Miss Congreve home.'

Charles regarded him sardonically. 'Yes, I daresay you would.'

'Silly,' said Julia. 'If my friend is unwell, I would naturally go back with her myself, but I thank you very kindly for your offer.'

'And as I am quite recovered, the question does not arise,' said Verity. She then felt ashamed of herself for being snappish as she remembered Charles had a full day in his chambers ahead of him tomorrow. She laid a hand on his arm. 'I am grateful for your concern, but I assure you I am well able to sustain myself for the length of a rubber of piquet.'

Charles gave her the merest lift of an eyebrow before turning to Lord Fitzgilbert. 'Then I accept your sister's offer with pleasure, if it suits you.'

Lilith's brother shrugged. 'It is a sight more pleasant playing cards than it is listening to wandering pipes and impassioned poetry. A penny a hundred suit you? I should not like to fleece you on my own property.'

Good, now Verity could observe Lieutenant Neville and his interactions with Julia properly. She settled down to so, but was thwarted when he rose to his feet and sauntered towards the card room likewise. Two of the others followed. Lieutenant Crisp flushed unhappily and made to rise. Julia put a playful hand on his arm. 'I cannot have my whole escort abandoning me for the baize. Tell us more about your foreign manoeuvres. Is it safe, yet, to go to France? I have heard one can now take tours of the battlefields, which I cannot help considering a little lacking in respect. What do the army think of them?'

8

Verity gave up the unequal struggle for sleep at dawn. She felt out of sorts after the soiree and needed the company of ordinary people to balance her. The view from her window, showing a maid scurrying by with a basket and an early morning street sweeper, were soothing. A cart delivering coal plodded past, reminding her of Charles's task yesterday. Never had she found herself more in charity with his work. How did Lilith stay so detached in the face of the privileged foolishness of her stepmother's circle? How did Julia find sufficient to occupy her in the intrigues and scandals of society? At least Verity's mind was now at rest about Julia herself. She had not caught her before they retired last night, but if Lieutenant Neville knew so little of her friend as to be passing her notes, she was not in danger. They would talk properly this morning, just as soon as Verity had been out long enough to shake the fidgets from her reasoning. When her maid came in with the washing water, she declared that they would go shopping before breakfast for the handkerchiefs she'd previously forgotten. Bridget laid out a walking dress, hoping aloud that they would not be long. She did seem pale and heavy eyed, but Verity reassured her that she would make her purchases in no time.

Outside, the air was still, with an acrid tang of smoke to it. 'Newton's, Coventry Street,' she said briskly to the driver of the first hackney cab they encountered. She formed no great opinion of the horse, who would have been laughed off the streets of Newmarket, but tipped the man an extra tuppence when she alighted, recommending him to spend it on a good bucket of hot mash for the beast, such as her father's head groom had often advised. 'For she'll be of no use to you dead,' she pointed out. 'Even my brother sees to his cattle before himself, and he is the most selfish man imaginable.'

'Yes, miss.' The man nodded with the weary obedience that comes from having so many cares he could no longer think straight. The gesture was like a slap in the face.

'Oh, forgive me,' said Verity, horrified and contrite. 'As if you do not know that. I am so sorry for my presumptuousness. Will you wait for me here, please? I will not be above quarter of an hour. When we are back I can send you to the livery stables my Godmama uses, with a note that feed for your horse is to be added to Mr Congreve's account.'

'I'll wait, miss. God bless you.'

Inside Newton's, Verity quickly perceived the counter she required and moved towards it. Though it was early, there were already a large number of customers in the shop. She sent Bridget back to wait in the cab and applied herself to the task of pushing between people to check on the quality of the goods. She had almost made her choice when a shout went up further along the counter.

'Oi! Stop thief!'

Verity looked around, startled. It was the duty of the public to apprehend any thief. A child whisked past her legs, the telltale corner of a new handkerchief peeking out from a ragged waistband. *A handkerchief.* Yesterday's dreadful scene at the Old Bailey came back to her. Quicker than thought, Verity tripped the boy, extracted the square of linen and bent, saying, 'You poor child, I am so sorry to have stepped into your way. Dear me, you have hurt yourself.' The handkerchief she contrived to ball up and throw several feet along the floor, proffering her embroidered one to glean the graze.

'Young varmint. Your pardon, miss, but he ain't worth spilling tears over. It's off to the rotation house with him. I'll give him in charge myself.'

Verity opened her eyes wide at the

sales assistant who came puffing out from behind his counter to haul the child up by his ragged collar. 'The rotation house?' she said. 'For what crime?'

'Are you simple, miss? For stealing that there handkerchief.'

'But this is my own. I gave it to him. See — there are my initials. He appears to have nothing else on him.'

The man glowered and relaxed his hold on the boy. 'You're lucky this time. I'll have you though. I'll have you. What have you done with it, eh? There's one missing from my pile.'

Further along in the shop a voice said, 'Here is a handkerchief. Here on the floor.'

'There,' said the assistant triumphantly. 'What did I say? He dropped it when I spotted him. Come along with me, my lad. I can't sell it now, so I'll have the cost out of your hide.'

'I do not think you can prove that,' said Verity, wrinkling her brow earnestly. 'Why, anyone might have knocked it off your counter. I might have done so myself while I was looking at them. To be sure it is a little dusty, but it is nothing that will not shake out.'

'Dusty and crumpled. It'll need cleaning before it's ... Oi, you little ... ' The child had seen his chance, jerked free and escaped. The assistant looked after him sourly. 'I'll get him next time. The sooner that one's in the colonies the better.'

'I daresay he was alarmed by the noise,' said Verity. 'Now then, how much will you reduce this handkerchief by? Having given mine away, I find myself without one. Shall we say fourpence if you are so sure it is ruined? I require black-edged handkerchiefs also. What do you have, please?'

The jarvey was waiting with Bridget when she emerged. They returned home where she wrote a note and asked the footman to give directions to the stable. She went upstairs to rouse Julia feeling very thoughtful.

'Good morning, Julia. I have asked for hot chocolate to be sent up. Do you wish me to read Lieutenant Neville's note or have you burnt it already?'

'Go away and let me sleep, Verity.'

'Certainly not. I want to talk to you. Really, Julia, whatever are you doing?'

Julia wriggled upright and reached for her wrapper. 'Saving Peter Crisp from ruin, as I promised his sister I would. You are a nuisance. I now owe Lilith sixpence. I thought it would take you a week to find out.'

'That is your own fault. You should have more faith in me. Talk.'

'It was at the Cattsons' house party in June. I'm sure I told you of it because we came back from Shropshire via Newmarket on purpose to persuade you both to London for a visit. Mary Cattson was very nearly involved in a scandal, but her father paid the man off; and apart from a little speculation amongst the house party when Mr North was found to have suddenly departed, it all came to nothing.

Indeed, there was more concern over the absence of the girl who brought the hot water up in the morning than there was over Mary. Everything was smoothed over most satisfactorily.'

'And nobody knew but you,' said Verity, 'because you always do know all the goings on, even in a large house.'

'People are interesting,' said Julia simply. 'Poor Mary. Mr North was so charming and with such an air, it was easy to see why he turned her head. The alliance would never have done though, for he was far older than her and not rich, I think.'

'Where does Lieutenant Crisp come into it? You didn't mention him to me in June.'

'Oh, nowhere. It was simply that Sukie Crisp was also at the house party. She told me her brother's regiment was back from Europe, but she was worried because from the tone of his letters, Peter seemed to have got in with a rogue set of officers. His company was due to move shortly to London, so I said I would do my best to run across him and turn his thoughts in a different direction.'

'You have succeeded. Very laudable, but he is a younger son, is he not? What were you planning to do when the poor man, who I daresay has only his pay to support him, declared himself hopelessly in love with you? It has happened before. I still remember the haberdashery assistant serenading you under our window at school. And the dancing master threatening to suicide himself in that dramatic French fashion of his.'

Julia smiled nostalgically. 'Happy days. But I was young and giddy then and know very much better now how little it takes to encourage the foolish creatures. I will tell Peter I am very fond of him, but firstly I have no money, and secondly my heart is unswervingly fixed on another.'

'And him so besotted, he'd believe you. What of Lieutenant Neville? How does he figure in this pretty scenario?'

'He is the rogue influence. I have not

yet discovered his intent.'

Verity raised her eyebrows. 'I would say his intent is obvious to the meanest intelligence.'

A faint blush spread over her friend's countenance. 'I am not yet so bored as to be lost to reason, Verity.' She reached across to rummage in her reticule. 'Here is his note.'

Verity unfolded the scrap of paper. '*Park. Two p.m.* Very enigmatic. Do you intend to meet him?'

'Naturally not. That would be the height of foolishness.'

'This is a dangerous game you are playing.'

'I said I was bored. Drink your chocolate and let me bathe and dress in peace. Mama and I are bidden to my great-aunt today. It will be enormously tedious, but she was kind to Mama in her younger days and these visits must be made. You and your mother can amuse yourselves, I daresay?'

'Nothing easier. I will see you at dinner.' She kissed her friend and left.

Mrs Bowman however, when asked how she would like to spend the morning, was found to have a headache and unequal to any exertion. Verity suspected Charles would be unimpressed by a second unheralded descent on his chambers, so resigned herself to a day of correspondence and the mending of her old gloves. She had just completed this depressing task when the footman brought a short note from Charles himself.

'*Scrivener has discovered a Captain Eastwick living in Henrietta Street. I am able to escort you there on Friday, if you wish.*'

Verity immediately penned a reply accepting the offer, wishing that the underlying feeling of satisfaction emanating from Charles's neat lines was because they were making progress, not because he saw a possibility of sending her back to Newmarket post-haste once Kitty was found. She had by no means achieved all her objectives in coming to the capital yet.

It occurred to her that Henrietta Street contained Bedford House, where linens and cottons could be got remarkably cheaply from Messrs Layton & Shears. It also occurred to her that if she and Mama *did* take Furze House, it would require a deal of new curtaining. There would be no harm, surely, in taking a preliminary look at what might be available?

After conscientiously asking her mother if she wished to come with her and receiving a faint shudder in reply, Verity set forth.

It was gloomy outside, with a stuffy feeling to the air. The smell of smoke from earlier increased the further they progressed. Her maid was quiet and Verity remembered with a stab of remorse that she had not felt well that morning. Sure enough, they had no sooner reached their destination than the generally stoical Bridget turned green and mumbled that she was sorry, miss, but she was really very ill. Verity sent her back in the hackney with instructions to go to bed, assuring her that she would be perfectly all right in the warehouse on her own. She wanted merely to form an idea of what was available and reckon up the likely cost. This exercise would have the dual effect of proving to Charles both her rationality of purpose and the seriousness of her intention in moving their establishment away from the dower house.

Buoyed up by these righteous thoughts, Verity entered the establishment of Layton and Shears where the bolts of material were so tempting that, without at all meaning to, she bought a length of Italian silk in lilac and another of deep pink sarsenet faster even than Julia would have managed. She could hear her friend's voice in her head saying the pink would be perfect for when she came out of mourning and indeed she need not wait the full period, for hadn't Verity's Uncle James always been uncomplimentary about sombre colours on young ladies?

Uncle James. The legacy. Recollecting herself with a guilty start, she hurriedly immersed herself in the rival merits of brocade and damask with only stray, longing glances at the satins and gauzes. Eventually, with all her sums done and a length of figured cotton added as a reward, she gathered up parcels and samples and left the shop.

The street was now quite misty. Conscience-stricken about how long she had been in Bedford House, Verity walked down the road a little way to hail a hackney. She looked keenly at the houses as she passed, wondering which one might be Captain Eastwick's address. There was quite a press of people towards the corner of the road. She edged through them, wishing she was tall enough to see over the heads. A phaeton bowled past at far too fast a lick in the poor light. The crowd swayed, grumbling. To her horror, Verity saw a small girl lose her footing and fall towards the road where a second phaeton was galloping after the first, evidently with the aim of overtaking it. Without thinking, she lunged forward to catch the child. As she pulled her to safety, the girl looked up, bewildered and scared. Her elfin face, dark hair and grey eyes were so familiar that Verity gasped.

'Kitty?' she said. 'But how can you be?'

'Ann,' shouted a frantic voice behind them. 'Ann, where are you?'

'Mama . . . ' called the child, a quaver to her voice.

A woman pushed through to Verity's side and scooped the little girl up. 'Oh thank you. I saw the phaeton and . . . Verity! Oh my . . . Verity, is it really you?'

Joy broke in Verity's chest and spilled out in a torrent of words as she embraced her sister. 'Kitty. I've been looking for you. Oh, this is too ridiculous. To find you here! I cannot believe it. How long has it been?'

'Too long. Much too long. Verity, I

. . . oh, there are no words . . . ' Kitty — older, more fine-drawn, but undoubtedly her own beloved sister — cast a distracted look at the crowded street. 'We cannot talk here. Will you step along to my house? It is not far, and we will be quite undisturbed.'

'How can you even ask? I should like it above all things. Kitty, I don't know what I am saying or doing. I'm so happy.'

It seemed to take no time at all before they had hurried back up Henrietta Street and were two flights above the street in Kitty's small, neat set of rooms, side by side on a sofa with Ann clutched against her mother next to them.

Still half-dazed with wonder and happiness, Verity could not get enough of Kitty's face. 'Have you been in London all this time?' she asked. 'I could have come to see you so often when I was visiting Julia. Mama will be happier even than me. I must tell her as soon as I return. She was ill with worry for you when you left, though she hoped, of course, that you would be happy. We have both missed you so. Will you come with me to see her now? We are staying in Grosvenor Street with the Congreves. You remember Julia, I am sure.'

'I . . . yes, I remember, and now I remember your tumble of words which I had forgotten. It is as if you have grown up — and not grown at all. Verity, I hardly know what I am saying in the astonishment of seeing you again, but I cannot come. She will not welcome me. She never answered any of my letters. I do not blame her, for I behaved very wrongly, but I was dazzled and wilful and I could *not* have married Mr Prout. Or so I thought then. Now, I . . . No matter, we will not talk of it. I made my own bed and cannot go back. Is she well? I wish she would at least see Ann.'

Verity stared at Kitty in consternation. 'She will see you both. Of course she will. Kitty, we never received any letters. How could you think for a single moment that we would not have answered, had we known where you were?'

The heartbreak in her sister's eyes at this statement was almost more than she could bear. 'My father suppressed them,' said Kitty bleakly. 'I was a fool to think I could cross him without retribution.'

'He died this spring. Did you not realise when you saw us at John's wedding? We were hardly in festive garb. That *was* you outside St George's?'

Kitty ducked her head. 'I saw the notice and went out of curiosity, telling myself it must be some other John Bowman. I looked, saw you all, then lost my nerve and hurried away.'

'It matters not.' Verity hugged her sister again, hiding her dismay at how thin and brittle Kitty felt. 'You are here and I have found you and I have a new niece whom I love already and you will both come to see Mama with me.'

'Yes. Yes, but . . . ' Kitty broke off as rapid footsteps were heard outside the door. Her animation drained away. Once again, Verity saw hard-won maturity in her expression, together with rapid, wary calculation. 'It is Simon. I did not expect him yet. Something has happened. You must go, Verity. I cannot explain now. Follow my lead.'

The door burst open without ceremony and Captain Eastwick hurried in.

Verity was instantly engulfed in memory. He filled the room, as he always had. His was a personality that would always take centre stage and make it his own. She remembered all over again why she hadn't felt the least surprise when Kitty eloped.

Right now Simon Eastwick emanated urgency. 'Devil take it, there was a fire in Hart Street last night and now the fog is thickening. Did you not hear of it when you went out? Why did you not tell me? It is too late by far to do anything at this distance. All are long scattered and there is little hope of finding . . . ' He broke off, his eyes going to Verity. 'Well, Kit, who have we here? Who is the fair visitor?'

Follow my lead, Kitty had said, but Verity also saw the suspicious flash of almost-recognition in Kitty's husband's gaze and she felt Kitty herself begin to frame a lie.

Instinct took her. She put out a hand and said with the utmost friendliness, 'Captain Eastwick. I daresay you won't remember me, but I remember you very well. I am Verity Bowman. I was Kitty's schoolgirl sister when you were courting her. Oh, the number of times I hung out of the window and sighed over your red coat and elegant address.'

Yes, he was as handsome and mesmerising as ever, but Verity was seven years more discerning now and she could see in his bearing how he traded on his looks.

Conceit puffed out his chest at her

words. An expression of good humour replaced the speculation. He shook her hand a little too heartily. 'Well, well, little Verity. Grown up just as comely as your sister. As you see, Kit and I rub along pretty well. How did you find us, eh? Last I heard, your father was ready to take a horsewhip to me for stealing away the prettiest girl in Newmarket.'

'Oh, it was the most absurd thing. I had been in Bedford House and was on my way back when I saw a little girl the image of my lost sister trip by the side of the road. I naturally put out a hand to save her and found she was a niece I did not know I possessed! Such a happy chance, was it not?'

'Indeed.'

Verity could not quite like the conjecture working in the back of his gaze, but she pretended to notice nothing amiss and stood in a flurry of cloak, gloves and parcels as unlike herself as she could manage. 'I must be leaving, for I am later than I said I would be. It was so nice to find you,

Kitty. I hope we may meet again.'

'Certainly,' said Captain Eastwick. 'Certainly you should meet with your sister. Family are always welcome provided there are no horsewhips present, eh Kit?'

Kitty smiled and laughed, but she was evidently hiding her unease. She embraced Verity, murmuring, 'Newton's in Coventry Street, ten o'clock tomorrow.'

Verity managed to give the tiniest nod before she was ushered out of the door.

9

Outside, Verity found with no little dismay that the fog had thickened and the sky was darker. The door had already shut behind her. 'What of it?' she said to herself. 'I am not so poor a creature as needs a footman or maid to hail a hackney cab. If I turn towards Southampton Street where the road is wider, and then go on to the Strand, it will be easier to see, I am sure.'

Which she did, but then caught sight of a bonnet shop on the corner of an alley and just stepped down that way for a moment to look at the window. She was sure, quite sure, that she turned in the correct direction when she'd regretfully decided against an Angouleme at this stage in her mourning, but soon found herself bewildered by the streets and turned first one way, then the other until her sense of direction was quite confounded.

She stopped, alarmed at the loud thumping of her heart in her ears. 'This is foolish,' she said, striving for calm. 'I can only be a turn or two away from a main thoroughfare. It is simply this wretched mist confusing me. If I could but make out my surroundings, I'd be out of this fix in a trice.' But the tall terraced buildings, their top storeys indistinct in the fog, crowded her reason, making a mockery of her senses. She heard brisk footsteps of somebody who certainly knew where they were and spun towards them thankfully, discerning the shape of a woman approaching. 'Pray excuse me, but could you help me, please? I fear I am lost.'

'You must be, if you're down here alone. Wait, I know your voice, don't I?'

'Is . . . is that Molly Turner? I met you in Bow Street . . . goodness, was it only yesterday morning? I was so glad when you were acquitted.'

'Bless me, you gave me your fichu!

Well, it's turn and turn about as they say. I'll see you safe, miss. Where was you wanting to get to?'

Oh, the relief. Verity thought she had never been so glad to hear a friendly voice before. 'That is very kind. I don't wish to take you out of your way. If I can but find a hackney cab, I can take it to Grosvenor Street.'

'You walk along with me. I'm on my way to the theatres. Custom's always good there, even as early as this, and there are generally a few coaches looking for a fare. It's a bad day to be out, that's for sure. I'd rather be in front of my own grate, but work is work and I've no money for enough candles for my sewing, so needs must, eh? The nippers will be all right with Ma, sorting tomorrow's laundry. It's not what I like, but there. You've got to eat, haven't you?'

'Yes indeed,' said Verity, having only the haziest idea what Molly was talking about, but wanting to sound sympathetic in case she offended her and

145

suddenly found herself alone again.

Molly set a good pace. The mist deadened their footsteps and the damp seemed to creep around the edges of Verity's cloak as they hurried along. She suspected if she asked what sort of work Molly was heading for, she might well be embarrassed by the answer, so instead said, 'Do you do much sewing? I always start with good intentions, but then I become impatient and my stitches get too long.'

'I do it when I can see to, miss. It's soothing, and there's a satisfaction in seeing something made good again. The way I came to it was this: Ma's taken in laundry all her life and we children got put to the tub as soon as we could see over the rim. Well, sometimes there would be a seam gone in a shirt, or a hem pulled that needed a stitch or two. It's all extra pennies, isn't it? I realised early on that if I did the mending nice and neat I'd be given more of it and less of the scrubbing, and that would mean I'd be sitting down, not standing, and it'd be a deal kinder on my hands than having them in water all the time.'

Verity was impressed by the cheerful practicality of her companion. 'That is very true.'

'Ma's hands and her cough are shocking. I'd dearly love to get her out of London and into the country air but there, it's what we've always known and it's a reasonable life so long as folk pay up. Can't boil the copper without coin for coal, can you? It's a funny thing, the richer folk are, the longer they leave their bills before settling up. That's what I like about evening work, you get your money straight away and sometimes a bite of supper too. They don't want those sort of dockets being sent to the house, do they?' Molly seemed more amused than embarrassed.

'Er, no.'

Molly chuckled. 'I lost my patience with the longest-running of Ma's laundry bills and started going around to the back of the big houses asking to speak to the butler in person. Amazing how it brought forth the readies.'

All the time they had been talking, Verity had been aware of other pedestrians in the fog, most muffled to the ears, some walking past with head down against the mist, occasional silent figures skulking around corners like oozing patches of murk. Now a bigger shape loomed out of an alley, turned at the sound of Molly's laugh and made straight for them, the scent of ale on his breath.

'What have we here? A pretty pair for plucking, I say.'

The man's voice was rough. Verity instinctively shrank against Molly.

'You don't want to bother with us,' said her new friend comfortably. 'We're on a different path tonight.'

'Is that so? Who's to say it's not mine? I might walk that way myself.' Verity could hear the leer in the man's words and had to guard against the nausea in her throat. She gripped her parcels to stop her hands shaking.

Molly, however, lost not an ounce of

confidence. 'It wouldn't be very smooth, I'm afraid. Our way is paved with flint.'

'That's different. I'll leave you then.' The alteration in the man's attitude was palpable as he swerved away towards a narrow opening where a dim light indicated an ale-house and noise came faintly through the fog.

Molly let out a silent breath and picked up her pace.

'What did you mean by that?' Verity asked, scurrying alongside her, curious about the deliberate phrasing she'd used.

Molly hesitated. 'It's by way of being a safe word, miss, but it don't do to use it often in case you get taken up on it. Pray you'll never know why. I had a friend once who . . . well, never mind that. How did you find yourself here? You're a world away from Grosvenor Street.'

'It was the stupidest thing. I was leaving Kitty's house in Henrietta Street and I must have missed my turning in the fog.'

'Kitty Eastwick?' Now Molly's voice was sharp. 'One of Sim's fancies, are you? Who'd have thought it? I might have spoken truer than I knew.'

'I'm sorry, I do not understand. Kitty is my sister. We lost touch and I have only just discovered her again, so was paying her a visit.'

'Ah, that's the way of it. I must say, you don't look much like her, but there's something in your manner of talking that reminds me of when I first knew her. Well, here's Drury Lane and here's a hack. I see you, Fred Grimes. You take this lady where she wants to go or I'll know about it.'

'Who's that? Molly Turner? Damn this fog. Horse can't hardly see her own feet. I'll take her if you'll sit up here alongside and keep me warm. It's a raw day. Be better with you tucked under my coat.'

'And what time do I have to go riding? That won't pay the rent or put broth on the table. In you get, miss, he talks a fine line, but he'll see you right.'

Verity fumbled in her reticule. 'Please, Molly, I am so grateful for your help. I would have been quite undone had I not met you. Will you take this with my thanks?'

She was worried she might offend the other woman, but Molly simply gave the coin a professional glance before it disappeared into her clothing. 'Bless you, miss, you're welcome, I'm sure. I've no need to work tonight now. That's twice I'm indebted to you. Grosvenor Street, you say? I'll ride along of Fred like a lady then. Neither of us will be the worse for a cosy-up and to tell the truth, I'll be glad not to stand around in the cold and damp this evening.'

'Grosvenor Street?' said the jarvey suddenly. 'Why didn't you say so right off? I was wanting to thank you for your kindness to my poor horse. Made all the difference to her, that mash. I doubt we'd be out here now without it.'

'Oh is it you? I apologise for not

recognising you. I'm so glad it helped. Do go in again and tell them I sent you.'

Now she was safe, Verity began to feel worse by the minute. She couldn't shake off her fright at how tall and narrow and menacing the streets had seemed to become in the fog. The thoughts of those slinking shadows and the roughly spoken man and what might have befallen her had Molly not had such presence of mind made her tremble so hard she could hardly open the door when they stopped.

Fortunately, it was opened for her. Unfortunately, it was opened by Charles in as towering a rage as she had ever seen him.

'Where have you *been*?' he said furiously.

It was like a draught of strong medicine. Verity's agitation was instantly swept away. Charles's exasperated anger was so much a part of every escapade she and Julia had embarked on in their younger days that it restored the balance in her world as nothing else could have done. She scrambled up to the driver's perch and embraced Molly, before paying Fred Grimes and reminding him about the mash. Only then did she submit to being hustled into the house and facing the full force of Charles's displeasure.

'Where have you been?' he repeated. 'The footman tells me you sent your maid home above three hours ago. Have you no idea of the dangers facing an unaccompanied young lady in London? Especially in this weather. And now I find you taking an affectionate leave of a jarvey's woman! I ask you, is this rational behaviour, Verity? Would this find favour with your uncle?'

'It started entirely rationally,' she protested, divesting herself of her parcels. 'Charles, I have so much to tell you that I scarce understand it myself, but Mama is unwell, so I must first set her mind at rest. Also, I am cold and damp and I have had a horrid fright and if I do not get some bread and butter and something warm to drink inside me this instant, I will forget everything and never remember it in the right order.'

'Then by all means let us bespeak tea,' said Charles with awful politeness. 'I would by no means wish to miss a single minute of today's doings.'

The footman winked at Verity in sympathy and effaced himself in the direction of the kitchen. Verity took a deep breath and followed Charles to the drawing room, stopping with him on the threshold in astonishment as he opened the door.

'Mama,' she said faintly.

'Sir,' said Charles, equally astounded.

Her mother, far from being prostrate on the couch with a sick headache, was cheerfully dispensing tea from Mrs Congreve's nicest silver pot and laughingly inviting an animated Mr Tweedie to partake of another slice of cake.

★ ★ ★

Two minutes earlier, Charles had been consumed by a maelstrom of strong emotion: anger at Verity for being so thoughtless, fear as to what might have been, relief that it hadn't, panic about what had given her a fright and anger again at himself for not being able to keep his feelings under control. Now however, sheer surprise swamped everything.

'Ah, Charles,' said his senior partner, peering over his spectacles, 'and Miss Bowman. There you both are. As you see, I have accepted Mrs Bowman's kind invitation to call. We were just exchanging recollections of the late admiral.'

As Mr Tweedie's most recent animadversions on Mrs Bowman's brother would have made even the most clear-sighted sister bridle, Charles was left with precisely nothing to say to this.

'Did you find any suitable samples?' asked Mrs Bowman at the same time.

'George thinks your notion of us removing to Furze House is an excellent one. He is sure that with a little application, John might release me an annual sum to reflect the convenience of him having the dower house back in his own hands to use for staff quarters, or to let.'

Charles looked at Mr Tweedie, aghast. Had the man taken in none of his concerns about Verity being let loose on the wider world without even her brother close by as a brake?

His partner polished his glasses and beamed back at him affably. 'You can make an appointment with Bowman's attorney tomorrow to set the process in motion,' he said.

'Certainly,' said Charles with only the merest hint of gritted teeth. He turned to Mrs Bowman. 'It is a pleasure to see you looking so well, Mrs Bowman.'

'We have been talking of the old days. I had quite forgotten some of the adventures my brother got up to.'

'No, did he really?' said Verity, sitting

down and looking up at Charles with a rueful, quicksilver smile that said they would have to put off their argument for later so he might as well make himself comfortable. 'And him making me that absurd condition that I must be rational for six months before I inherit. How very hypocritical of Uncle James.'

'Possibly he was remembering *your* younger days,' muttered Charles, taking a seat next to her.

'I don't see how he would have known about them unless you told him,' retorted Verity under her breath as she bent to rearrange her skirts.

She poured them both tea and began to draw her mother out on the subject of her uncle's wild past. Charles listened, resigned to the familiar sensation of his infuriation draining away, smiling despite himself at her skill in integrating his senior partner into the conversation.

The cake had all been eaten and the tea tray removed before Mr Tweedie glanced at the clock on the mantelshelf and gave an astonished start.

'Bless my soul, is that clock quite right? I had no idea of staying so long. I fear I have been imposing on your good nature.'

'Not at all,' protested Mrs Bowman. 'I have not had such an enjoyable afternoon for an age. But Verity, surely it is very late for your godmother and Julia to still be out? I hope nothing has happened to them.'

Charles crossed to the window where the curtains had been drawn against the fog. 'They were spending the day with my great-aunt, were they not?' he said, looking out at a mass of solid grey. 'If Richmond is as beset by fog as we are here, they will have delayed their departure. Do not distress yourself, Mrs Bowman. I feel sure they will stay overnight rather than take unnecessary risks with the horses.' He turned to his partner. 'I had best see you home, sir. It is not an evening for travelling alone.'

Verity looked up in dismay. 'Oh, but you will return to dine, will you not? I have to tell you about . . . about the programme Lilith and I have devised.'

Charles hesitated, torn. Clearly she had something to report beyond a mere explanation of her activities this afternoon. *I have had a horrid fright*, she'd said. Normally, that intelligence alone would make him stay. However, thieves and ruffians delighted in weather such as this, and Mr Tweedie was not a young man. Charles felt duty bound to escort him to his rooms. He glanced again at the clock. His own father would no doubt be dining at the House, and his mother had taken several of the grooms and footmen with her, so he was equally obliged to augment the male presence in Grosvenor Street until his father should return.

The matter was settled, surprisingly, by Mrs Bowman. 'You must both stay to dine,' she said. 'We can be quite informal, you know, and I am sure it is what your mama would wish, Charles. I confess to feeling some agitation about her. The presence of *two* gentlemen in the house will allay both Verity's fears and my own.'

Mr Tweedie needed very little pressing to accept. Mrs Bowman called the footman in to explain and said she would personally usher Mr Tweedie to a spare room that he might refresh himself. Charles and Verity were left alone.

10

Charles turned to Verity, conscious of a reluctance to spoil the camaraderie of the last hour. 'What was is it you wished to tell me?'

'Oh, so much, Charles. Some of it might have been a little foolish, so please, you will not shout at me so very loud and bring the servants in?'

'I shall attempt to restrain myself,' he promised, shaken by the troubled look on her face. 'Come and tell me. Why, for instance, were you out quite alone?'

As she poured out the circumstances of Mrs Bowman's headache that had evidently passed, Bridget's illness, Bedford House, the crowd, the phaeton race and the little girl falling, Charles was visited by the habitual creeping disbelief at how these things always happened to Verity. Then she reached

Kitty, and Kitty's husband, and his attention sharpened. By the time she had got to Molly Turner and the walk through thick fog in one of the more notorious parts of London, he had ceased to smile at all.

'God's tears, Verity, do you know how lucky you were?'

'I didn't then, but telling it over, I do now,' she said in a small voice. 'I'm sorry, Charles. This is worse than the time Julia and I set the bear free because we felt sorry for it being chained at the fair, isn't it?'

'It approaches it. If you see your friend Molly again, which I devoutly hope and pray you will not, but from previous experience you probably will, you may tell her she has an attorney for life.'

'It was that bad?'

'It could have been. And yes, I do see, as you are about to observe, that one instance led to another and you could not have done anything else. You might, however, have asked them in

Layton & Shears to hail a hackney for you.'

'But then I should not have met Kitty! I realise now I should have taken more notice of her house. Or I should perhaps have requested that Captain Eastwick set me on the right road back.'

Cold shot through Charles. 'No,' he said slowly. 'No I begin to believe not doing that may have been one of your better decisions.'

She slanted an intelligent look up at him. 'Is it because of what Molly said? He is one of those who dominates any room he is in. I own I did not feel comfortable with him. Something had evidently happened to overset him because he was very agitated when he first came through the door. The change on seeing me was quite remarkable.'

'You are quick. Yes, there are two things your Molly said that interest me considerably.'

'I am to meet Kitty tomorrow

morning. I can ask her for Molly's direction.'

Charles made an involuntary movement of protest. 'I cannot stop you seeing your sister, Verity, but neither do I like the scheme. The fact that she is uneasy enough about her situation to propose the meeting in a clandestine manner bothers me a great deal.'

'But Charles, I must see her again. I want her and Ann to come back with us to Newmarket.'

'You cannot abduct a man's wife and child, however good your intentions and however dubious you suspect that man to be.'

'I can suggest it to her though. And Charles, I think you want to talk to her, do you not? Her and Molly both.'

'Dammit, Verity, how do you do that?'

She laid a hand on his. 'Because I am not stupid. Do you think we women never talk together? I learnt from Jenny months ago about you winning Adam Prettyman's West Indian actor at cards and setting him free. Even before we went to Bow Street, I knew you did other work away from Mr Tweedie's chambers. There has always been a passion for justice within you, Charles. When we were growing up I heard how you thrashed Edward Coalville when he took a stick to the boot boy. That was not the only time you insisted on righting wrongs yourself. It makes me annoyed when people disparage you for being 'just an attorney' when there is very much more to you than that. If you wish to pretend otherwise, then by all means do so, but do not expect me to fall in with it. Do not prevent me playing my part to help.'

'Even though you were frightened today?'

'*Because* I was frightened today. I do not like to think other ladies might also feel like that, and with better reason.'

Charles felt a helpless rush of admiration for this infuriating, head-strong, naive-yet-knowing girl. No, not a girl. She was a woman grown.

'May I accompany you to Newton's tomorrow?' he said at last. 'I will not interfere with your conversation, but I should like very much to know if anyone is watching your sister. And if they are, I would not entirely object to them knowing you yourself have a protector.'

'Thank you,' she said meekly. 'Would you also like me to write a note to Lilith, asking that her brother accompany us to Somerset House tomorrow afternoon?'

He spread his hands in exasperation. 'It seems you know my business better than I do. By all means let Fitz and I be bored together.'

She gave him an impish smile. 'Then I shall do so. Heavens, we had best wash. Mama and Mr Tweedie will be down soon to dinner. Do you think he will be scandalised if I change into a gown with a little more colour? I believe I will still be able to smell the fog on this one if Bridget airs it for a week.'

'I am perfectly sure he will think you

charming whatever you wear.'

'You have been *very* nicely brought up, Charles,' said Verity. 'Thank you for listening to me. You have no notion how much better I feel.' She squeezed his hand and kissed him lightly on the cheek before hastening upstairs.

Charles sat a moment more on the sofa. His hand crept to his face as if to imprison the gossamer touch. *Oh Verity. Oh Lord. Now what do I do?*

⋆ ⋆ ⋆

Dinner was over, backgammon had been played, tea had been drunk and Charles was only waiting for his father before escorting Mr Tweedie home through the fog. He had, considered Verity, been thoroughly amiable throughout the evening. She had been particularly diverted by the polite determination of both gentlemen to beat the other hollow at backgammon whilst deprecating the sad fall of the dice on their opponent's part.

A confusion of noise at the front door announced not only Mr Congreve's arrival, but also that of Mrs Congreve and Julia. It appeared Charles's father had gone to Richmond for the express purpose of escorting his wife and daughter home. Amidst the lamentations regarding the weather and the protestations of gratitude for their rescue from dullness, Verity found her hand being pressed by Charles with a murmured confirmation that he would be here in the morning for their appointment.

'I will be ready,' she promised. 'Thank you for staying. I enjoyed the evening, but I hope it did not put you out very much.'

He smiled. 'There was no way I would rather have spent the time.'

She followed her mother upstairs for the night, still delighted by the change in her. 'That was such a pleasant evening, Mama,' she said, perching on her mother's bed. 'I had no idea Mr Tweedie could be so entertaining.'

'He always was a dear man.'

'I have never seen you so cheerful either. You seemed almost translated.'

'I feel translated. I have remembered who I was.' Her mother sat in front of the mirror and looked at Verity in the glass with a kind of rueful wonder. 'So many years, Verity. So much weight on me, a layer at a time, I didn't even realise it was happening. Talking to George Tweedie has reminded me of the person I used to be.'

'The person you used to be when?'

'Before I married.' She turned, looking at her daughter directly. 'Mr Bowman was not my first choice as a husband. The gentleman George and I were speaking of this evening, your uncle's great friend, Will Lawrence. He and I were engaged. He was on his way to ask his grandmother if she would give us her blessing to make the betrothal public when ... ' Mrs Bowman broke off, then rallied. 'When he was set upon by highwaymen and killed.'

'Oh Mama . . . '

'After that, I did not care much whom I wed. Perhaps I should have held out a little longer but . . . your grandmother has a strong personality.'

It was the closest she had ever come to admitting she had made a mistake. Verity was forcibly reminded of Kitty's words. *I made my own bed.* 'Mama, I saw Kitty today,' she said abruptly. 'It was so unexpected. I am to meet her again tomorrow. I do not believe she is happy. May I try to persuade her to come to us?'

Mrs Bowman was pulled out of her reflections. 'Kitty? Why yes! A thousand times, yes. How did you come to meet her? Is she well?'

'I don't know. She is thinner and older, but still beautiful. She is warier than previously. I had very little time with her before Captain Eastwick came in. Mama, she has a little girl who looks just like her. She is called Ann.'

Verity's mother's hand went to her breast. Tears stood in her eyes. 'She named her daughter for me?' she whispered. 'Why, then, did she never write?'

'She says she did. I told her we did not receive the letters. Charles is to go with me in the morning to talk to her. I do not know if it will be possible, or even if she will want to, but I will bring her back if I can.'

*   *   *

'Kitty!'

'Verity. You came.'

'Not floods, snow or thunderstorms would have kept me away.' Even as she embraced her sister, Verity noticed how Kitty's wary gaze went to Charles. 'Do you remember Charles Congreve?' she continued. 'He insisted on accompanying me after my adventures yesterday. I will tell you about them presently.'

'I . . . yes. How pleasant to meet you again.'

Verity registered the scurry of calculation in her sister's face. Seven years had made so much difference. 'Mama begs that you come to her immediately, you and Ann, if you so wish. I did not ask yesterday, you have only the one child?'

'That is kind of her, more than I deserve. Yes, I only have Ann. I have quickened twice since bearing her, but . . . but it was not to be. I am not sorry for it. Ann's birth was very hard. Oh, how I longed for my mother then.'

'Then you will come?'

A shadow came over Kitty's face. Her arm tightened protectively around her daughter. 'I do not think I can,' she said in a low voice. 'Simon would find us. He cares little for me now, except as a convenience and to be useful, but he has a clear idea of what is his. Perhaps I might send Ann. I am fearful for her the whole time. I thought her too young for his schemes, but he has been in such a strange way recently that I believe he might grasp at anything.'

Charles spoke for the first time. 'If your husband is violent or cruel, you have the right to leave him.'

'Rights have very little place in Simon's world,' said Kitty bleakly. 'If we could escape clean away I would do so in a heartbeat, but he has acquaintance everywhere. He would find us. And then he would use Ann against me.'

Verity exchanged a troubled look with Charles. 'The offer remains open,' she said, 'and Mama does dearly wish to see you and Ann with as much dispatch as possible. Could I write a note asking you to call? Would it satisfy Captain Eastwick if I make it clear it is a social visit?'

Again there was deliberation in Kitty's eyes. 'I daresay I will pay for the privilege, but yes, an invitation has the most likely chance of success. I very much wish to see Mama again — and to ask her forgiveness.'

'Then I will do so as soon as I return. Oh, Kitty, I had such a foolish adventure yesterday. I turned wrong after leaving you and found myself quite lost in the fog. By the most fortunate chance I met a lady who put me right. Molly Turner, her name is. She said she knew you. I liked her enormously.'

Her sister's face lightened. 'Molly? Well, if that isn't just like you, Verity. You could not have found anyone better. Molly and her mother were my neighbours when I was in Water Street.'

Charles frowned at the name.

Kitty glanced at him quickly. 'You know the area? Yes, naturally you do. In those early years I became only too accustomed to moving from place to place in a quest for cheaper situations. Water Street was the worst. While we were there, Simon went away to find work. I was close to birthing Ann and frantic with fear — but Molly saw to all. She was with me throughout and showed me how to go on. I would have been dead without her and her mother, I am sure. I can never repay her. A month later Simon returned with money in his pocket and we moved to better rooms, but I remained friends with Molly.'

'As well you are not still there,' said Charles, a grim set to his voice. 'Even the authorities fear to go into the Alsatia district. It is a desperate place.'

'It is all of that. We have never been in quite such bad straights since. Simon follows a pattern of sorts. Every now and again he goes away for a few weeks and returns in funds. For a while he lives like a king and then he gambles it away. He is not a weak man, but everything is always the present with him. He has no notion of setting coin aside against the future. I learnt very soon never to scratch together any savings. He would take it and spend it and never think that there would be no money for food or coal. Now I keep just enough to live on, and instead lay in frippery.' She waved a hand at the counters around them. 'Small feminine items like handkerchiefs, ribbons, belts — little things that I can pawn for the price of a meal.'

'Is he in business?' asked Charles. 'He is evidently not a serving soldier.'

'No, he . . . he has interests that bring in money,' said Kitty. 'He does business near the docks. He buys and sells. He undertakes commissions. Sometimes these take him out of town. I don't ask about them. He . . . brings people together and he also has power over them.'

'Power?'

'Everything, every scrap of knowledge is currency in his book. He mines it, and reuses it. I told you he is a gambler. If he would only limit himself to cards we would be comfortable, for he is skilled at anything requiring memory and the foibles of others.' She grimaced. 'The men he plays with are not so fortunate. There have been many over the years. He has that air of dominance and recklessness that attracts followers. For a long while he would run card games at home, but he has been more particular these past several months about keeping his business away from the house. I do not know why, but I am grateful for it.' She swallowed. 'He thrives on victory. It was not pleasant to see his opponents crushed, handing over everything they possessed.'

Verity was feeling nauseous at the picture her sister painted. What a life Kitty must have been living.

Charles looked grave. 'Mrs Eastwick, you realise I am an attorney?'

Her expression was frank. 'I do. Your name is not unknown amongst my acquaintance. I wondered if you were the same Mr Congreve that Verity used to know, but I didn't see how you could be. *Pay-me-later*, they call you, do they not? I regret to say Simon thinks of you and your kind as saps, giving your time for no reward. I also know that even unpaid, you help those who are unable to help themselves. It is why I am talking so freely, though my own situation is beyond aid. I readily admit I was fascinated by Simon. I married him of my own free will so I have no rights, but I would be rid of this life, Mr Congreve. Scales fall slowly, but they do fall. I have done things out of desperation that I cannot relate out of shame. I thought there was no way out.'

'Kitty,' began Verity.

Kitty's face softened as she looked at her. 'That is what I *thought*. Then yesterday Verity appeared in front of me and cracked open a hole in my world. If there is a means of escape, and if above all things I can keep Ann safe, I will take it. It worries me, though, that Simon will hear of me talking to you, even here in a linen-draper's shop. He has eyes and ears everywhere and as I said, you are not unknown.'

'Then tell your husband the truth,' said Verity. 'That I have an inheritance from my uncle, but in order to receive it, I must prove to the executors that I can spend six months in a rational manner. Poor Charles, it is the greatest bore for him to be forced to accompany me on a daily basis. You can, perhaps, mention how irritable he looked as I pored over lengths of linen for curtaining or the table and what a waste of time he clearly thought it.' She smiled up at Charles as she spoke, and was amused to see him return her a haughty look.

'Tedious in the extreme,' he agreed. He dropped his voice. 'Mrs Eastwick, your friend Molly mentioned a certain word. A name, I believe it to be, though she did not say it as such. It is not in any way a condition on my helping you, but I would know more if it is in either your or her power to tell me.'

Kitty became a shade paler. 'I know very little except the name, but it is one my husband is chary of. Please, I cannot say more. No one can.'

'Then do not,' said Verity. 'I will write a note of invitation today. Call tomorrow, if you can. Mama is so much longing to see you and Ann.'

'I will. Now I have talked to you, I am determined. I will tell Simon I have hopes of her sponsoring Ann to an education such as your godmother gave you.' She gave a bitter laugh. 'It extends the fiction between us that all is well. I cannot stay talking longer. Ann and I must get to the market to bargain for ingredients for today's broth.'

'And I am being thrown fulminating glances from the clerk at the handkerchief counter,' said Verity. 'I helped a child escape yesterday. He had taken a handkerchief and I could not see him sent to the gallows.' She embraced her sister, feeling the thinness of her body and the sharp angles of her bones, and raised her voice. 'Dearest Kitty, so strange to see you again, twice in two days. I could talk forever, so much as we have to catch up on, but I am promised to my friend to see the paintings at Somerset House and we have already been out longer than I said.' She embraced Ann and then turned blindly to go.

Outside, Charles offered his arm. 'Verity?'

'I cannot abandon her. I cannot. We have to save her.'

His voice was strong and deep and utterly confident. 'We will.'

11

Somerset House was very grand and very chilly. Verity drew her pelisse more closely about her as they slowly traversed the first wall of the exhibition. 'You are looking beautifully bored, Charles,' she commented after a minute or so. 'Well done.'

'Save your praise for when I attempt something difficult,' he replied. 'I have rarely seen a more insipid set of portraits.'

'But many of them are of people we know,' protested Julia on his other side. 'I like them enormously. It's amusing finding what the *ton* consider to be the best costumes for portraits.' She moved away to inspect a particularly large specimen.

'I confess I find the artistic merits of satin versus Brussels lace tedious,' said Verity. 'I prefer to look at the visitors.

Why are there so many people here? They cannot *all* have nothing else to do.'

'This is a new collection,' said Lilith, sounding amused as she crossed the room to greet them. 'People are here to be seen. Good afternoon, Verity. Good afternoon, Mr Congreve. Yes, you may well look surprised at seeing both of us. My stepmother has a gentleman in to discuss 'improvements' she wishes to make to the orangery, so I have brought Benedict out to save him from the hangman's noose.'

The two men nodded to each other in a well-bred, long-suffering manner and fell behind as Lilith linked her arm in Verity's.

'Do you really come here for pleasure?' asked Verity.

'Frequently,' said Lilith. She glanced behind. 'Benedict, however, does not. I am intrigued to know how a word from you summoned him when I have been unable to persuade him to accompany me to a gallery these several years.'

'It is not me who is the attraction, but Charles,' said Verity. She paused in front of a soulful lady who had been painted against a background of a choppy sea and Grecian ruins. 'They have some sort of altruistic clandestine dealings which the polite world is not to know about. Hence his present portrayal of a conscientious attorney desperate for someone of intelligence to talk to. What does this signify, please? The poor woman looks frozen.'

'The ruins show the lady's classical leanings, and the sea indicates that her family made their money through trade. How very mysterious. I have long known my brother has interests that occasionally take him away, even beyond the natural desire to avoid my stepmother's environs at frequent intervals, but I didn't know what it was. Poor Benedict. He is far too much of a slave to convention for his own comfort. I wish he could fix on a lady to marry who is as politically minded as himself. He could then set stepmama up in her own villa without incurring the censure of my aunt and her circle, and we would all of us be happier.'

'Suppose you took your brother's new wife in dislike? It would be uncomfortable sharing a house, surely?'

'Not at all. I have managed to share with stepmama for five years without coming to blows. The trick is to agree to everything, then efface oneself and continue to do things in your own fashion, except I would no longer need to play the perfect hostess for Ben and could concentrate on my studies. Irritatingly, he has no need to marry for money, which would at least make him work at a relationship, and he is so intelligent that he is bored by all the chattering young ladies who contrive to be thrust under his nose by their mothers.'

Verity moved on to the next portrait, one that Julia was already conning with far more interest than she herself considered the subject warranted. 'These people are not at all true to life,' she complained. 'Everyone is rosy with health and beautifully dressed.'

'This is because painters must eat,' said Lilith with practical good sense. 'No one is going to commission an artist to create an unflattering image. For that you visit the print shops.'

Charles and Lord Fitzgilbert strolled up to them. 'I see you have found something worth studying, Julia,' said Charles.

'Yes indeed,' said Julia. 'I am trying to make out whether Mrs Hesketh is wearing the real Hesketh Emerald here, or whether it is a paste copy.'

Verity made an impatient noise. 'Julia, you cannot tell that from a painting! Any such indication is more due to the skill of the artist than the quality of the necklace.'

Benedict Fitzgilbert gave an amused snort. 'Miss Bowman is correct, but the jewel is paste for all that,' he said. 'The real emerald has done its family duty by shoring up Hesketh Castle and buying the eldest son a passage to New York, that he may hook himself an American heiress.'

Julia straightened up. 'Ah, thank you. That was what I had heard, but it is nice to have confirmation. Her wearing it is either bravado or pretence, then. Thank you so much for suggesting this, Lilith. I had no notion portraits could tell us so much about character.'

'And that is today's knowledge assimilated,' said Verity. 'What is through the arch? More portraits or something livelier?'

'Landscapes, I believe, with the odd battle at sea. Would you prefer them?'

Verity looked around in dissatisfaction. 'I would prefer something that was painted from the heart. Something like your sketches, Lilith. This is simply men showing off their wealth and importance by arraying themselves and their wives in costly fabrics and jewels. They are covering the cracks in their lives with deception.'

'You may make Admiral Harrington's

legacy over to Miss Bowman at once, Congreve,' said Lord Fitzgilbert. 'That is the most rational evaluation of the collection I've heard since I entered this benighted room.'

'Would that I could. Sadly, the estate requires proof, not mere sentiment. The Harrington family is breathing down my neck, just waiting for the slightest irregularity to challenge the will.'

'They will be satisfied by our performance today,' said Verity, 'even though you have led me wrong, Lilith. My uncle would not at all consider this a sensible use of my time. Unless the other room proves to be full of sea battles that I may learn something of history from, I think I would have preferred Bullock's Museum, which *was* a favourite of his.'

'I doubt you would have got my brother to Bullock's,' murmured Lilith under her breath. 'You forget, this exhibition is serving a dual purpose,' she went on aloud. 'You are also establishing yourself in society while you admire the skill of the artist. Everybody who is anybody is here.'

'Indeed,' replied Julia, 'and some of the visitors are more interesting than others.' Her eyes rested speculatively on a group of red coats just entering the gallery.

Verity saw Charles stiffen. 'Do you know everyone, Julia?' she asked hastily. 'Who is the supercilious man by the archway? The one in the elegant blue coat. I saw him at Bow Street. The clerks were so deferential it would have set my teeth on edge had it been directed at me, but he accepted it as his due and strolled out. I was never less taken with anyone.'

'Who do you mean? Oh, I see him. That is Sir Philip Munro. He has ten thousand a year and a house in Soho Square. One meets him in many places.'

'Why then is he a person of importance in Bow Street?' asked Verity.

'Because he is a gentleman thief-taker,' said Lilith's brother. 'He makes a great deal of ridding the streets of the criminal menace.'

Julia frowned at him, evidently picking up the flatness in his voice. 'So I understood. That is good, isn't it?'

'It would be if he not did puff off his own consequence by ostentatiously saying it was nothing. I would be more impressed if he brought in more of the rich thieves and fewer of the poor penniless embezzlers.'

'All of the glory, none of the substance,' murmured Charles. 'Which is doubtless very unfair of me. I have no personal knowledge of the man.'

'He has looked this way once or twice,' said Verity. 'I daresay he knows you by sight if you are often in Bow Street and wonders what you are doing here. Would you like me to be loud and effusive as we go past?'

'It is entirely your own decision,' said Charles, looking even more bored and raising his voice slightly as they left the others behind and walked through the arch. 'What were your uncle's opinions on the portrayal of sea battles? Did he consider them of educational value to the general populace?'

'Oh, assuredly, though he was inclined to be critical of the poor artists. I remember one time he spent quite half-an-hour in front of a large canvas pointing out that from the set of the sails on the ships in the painting, the wind appeared to be blowing from several different directions at once.'

There was only the slightest tremor in Charles's tone as he replied that no doubt the painter had not enjoyed the same degree of familiarity with the open ocean as the late admiral.

The circuit of the inner room was swiftly accomplished and they emerged again to find Julia paying court to her knot of officers. The group had been joined by various matrons and daughters whom Verity vaguely recognised, but as before, Julia was talking most animatedly to Lieutenant Crisp.

'Have you seen everything you

require, Julia?' asked Charles. 'I am loathe to disappoint your friends, but I have an appointment I must not miss.'

'I would be happy to escort Miss Congreve home if she wishes to stay longer,' said Lieutenant Crisp earnestly.

'And we would be happy to accompany him to ensure propriety,' drawled Lieutenant Neville.

'That does not sound so very proper,' said Verity. 'Are you enjoying the paintings? Do you know much about art?'

Lieutenant Neville's lazy gaze assessed and dismissed her.

Verity felt Charles's forearm muscles bunch under her hand. 'I believe we must *all* be going,' he said. 'Do pray stay and enjoy the collection, gentlemen. You seem to have remarkable amounts of leisure for officers of His Majesty's army. I am delighted to see you putting it towards an appreciation of culture.'

Lieutenant Crisp blinked at him, clearly not following the exchange.

Julia patted his arm kindly. 'Perhaps you could take Miss Everett around the paintings. She is so slight, I am worried she will become caught in the crush. I daresay I will see you at the rout next week. Charles, do wait until I have taken leave of Lilith. I shall not be above a minute.'

She darted off. Lieutenant Crisp crossed obediently to a slender brunette hanging on to her mother's arm. Lieutenant Neville watched Julia for a moment, then made some low-voiced comment to his companions who stifled their amusement.

Charles's eyes, however, were still on Lieutenant Crisp. 'I swear, Verity, if Julia runs off with that stripling, I will not rest until I have fetched her back.'

'She will not, though I can see you doing exactly that,' said Verity. She creased her brow. 'I have often wondered why my father would not go after Kitty and Captain Eastwick when they eloped. He rode roughshod over everything else. Every plan he made had to be carried out to the letter. Why would he not drag Kitty back to marry Mr Prout when the match was his own arrangement? It makes no sense.'

'Mr Prout?'

'He is a Newmarket gentleman with a small estate. Papa was most insistent on the match. They had dealings at the time, I remember. I believe Papa sold him a horse. Or Mr Prout sold Papa a dog. I don't recall the details.'

'I am ready,' said Julia, returning. 'That was a most instructive afternoon. Thank you so much for suggesting it, Verity. I cannot remember when I have enjoyed anything more, having started with such low expectations. Shall we go?'

* * *

On the way back, Charles let Verity's and Julia's chatter wash over him as he thought about the brief conversation he'd had with Fitz while both were striving to look as if they were mere nodding acquaintances.

'Interesting,' Fitz had said on being given a summary of Verity's adventures. 'I agree with you. A word with Molly Turner could be advantageous. An assignment for Nicholas, I think. He will be back tomorrow. If you start hanging around the theatres yourself, it could arouse suspicion in many undesirable quarters.'

'If *you* do, it will arouse even more. Nick, however, already has something of a reputation in that direction. Will you send him word?'

'I will. You concentrate on playing the conscientious attorney.'

'I *am* a conscientious attorney, and one who will have to work tonight to make up the time spent on this afternoon's charade. I apologise, by the way, for letting Verity know about us, but she had already guessed and as it turns out, her friendship with your sister is useful.'

His friend shrugged. 'Lilith is loyal and discreet. If you have no objection, she and Miss Bowman could form a useful line of communication.'

'It seems to have already been established.' Charles let his eyes rest on Verity's animated profile as she turned to ask something of Miss Fitzgilbert. 'This latest development shows promise, though I could wish Verity was not involved. A conversation with Mrs Eastwick regarding '*Sim's fancies*' might prove interesting, don't you think? Sadly, I do not see how I can be in Grosvenor Street the whole day waiting for her to call. I received all manner of curious looks in the haberdashery shop this morning as it was.'

'No matter. The information may come from Mrs Turner.'

'Or even from Verity herself. I swear these women pull information out of the air. Only collect two of them together and you have the secrets of three ducal houses laid bare in the same time that you and I could play a hand of piquet.'

'It's a thought, Charles.'

'No. No it isn't. We have both seen the bodies, Fitz.'

★　★　★

Now he left Verity and his sister in Grosvenor Street and proceeded to the Temple on foot, walking fast to shake the fidgets out of his body. In truth, he was not sorry to be on his own. That moment yesterday when she'd given him no more than a sisterly kiss . . .

He walked faster, rounding other pedestrians and the small knots of urchins who were everywhere on the streets. It was of no use him forming an attachment to Verity. He was a working attorney. He would not be able to give any woman a home for the next several years, much less the daughter of a gentleman who had been brought up with servants and space around her and a comfortable house. A voice in his head pointed out that he was a gentleman's son and that the rent on a set of rooms in the Albany was comparable with a small apartment in Islington, say, or a little further west. He told the voice to be quiet and turned into Middle Temple Lane almost at a run.

A soothing perusal of boundary clauses and the precise definition of a client's tenancy agreement did much to rid him of the sensation of a wasted afternoon, even if it failed to alleviate the disparity in his consciousness between a gentleman of means and a gentleman with no expectations whatsoever. He succeeded in writing several firm letters and sent them off with the clerk to the mail before he was informed that Scrivener was waiting, should it be convenient.

'Regarding Captain Eastwick,' began Scrivener, 'I collect Miss Bowman has now made contact with her sister.'

'She has, as have I this morning, but I should like to know more about the man himself.'

'I apprehended as much. His business dealings seem to mainly consist of moving money from one place to another, though little of it remains in his own pocket. A sight of his bank book shows occasional large sums deposited, coinciding with a period out of town, otherwise he lives from day to day, buying and selling around the docks and visiting discreet houses in Bloomsbury and Upper Church Street and rather less discreet ones in Hart Street, Drury Lane and the Haymarket. He also visits various gambling hells from Covent Garden to Shadwell. I have made a list of the addresses.'

Charles looked at the paper Scrivener placed in front of him. 'I wonder he finds the time. Does he frequent the tables in all these places?'

'He is of certainty a hardened gambler, but he appears selective in what and where he plays. At cards he generally wins. At dice he almost always loses. I have marked the establishments where he stays longest.'

'He visits, but does not always stay? The inference being that in some places he collects money, others he takes part in the play. Shadwell . . . ' He raised his eyebrows. 'I daresay the insalubrious location adds extra spice to the gentlemen who come to gamble there.'

'The ones who can afford to lose, yes. I understand the number of young men who take their own lives shortly after playing cards with Captain Eastwick is not insignificant.'

Another frisson of distaste rippled through Charles. 'Not only a card-sharp, but a murderer by extension. And according to his wife, caring for no one but himself, God rot him. Is there more to be found out? What is your next line of enquiry?'

Scrivener hesitated. 'Naturally I remain your humble servant and looked forward to future commissions, but on this occasion I would appreciate the balance of the fee and no more said on the matter.'

Charles looked at him shrewdly.

'Might I ask if you have a particular reason?'

'Let us say I have made the sort of enquiries any conscientious attorney such as yourself might order about an impressionable young client's relatives. To go further might invite the sort of attention one would rather not attract. Not if a person wishes to see their family grow to maturity and become settled in life.'

'You felt you were being observed?'

'I was aware of scrutiny, yes. Whether from Captain Eastwick's people or others, I could not say. I did not care to show I had noticed.'

Charles nodded. 'That seems wise. My thanks for continuing with the commission. Does the name Flint mean anything to you?'

'Geology has never been one of my interests,' said Scrivener firmly. 'Good day, sir.'

Alone, Charles read through the report with an increasingly grim set to his mouth. Much of it filled in the spaces which Kitty Eastwick had left. This constant perambulating between addresses . . . was Eastwick dealing in protection, rent, dividends or all three? Charles remembered Verity's half-sister from years back: the change between her vivid, beautiful wildness then and the wary, disenchanted woman in Newton's this morning, determined to protect her daughter at any cost to herself, made his stomach turn. She and Ann must be extracted from Eastwick as soon as possible. The question was, how to do it within the law? And how to keep them safe afterwards?

12

Verity found it difficult to settle on Saturday, so anxious was she to see Kitty. Eventually Julia commanded her to pass across the bonnet she was making a sad hash of trimming and instead to read *Glenarven* aloud so Julia could remind herself of all the delicious scandalous titbits in Lady Caroline Lamb's writing. Verity did so, but when the butler announced 'Mrs Eastwick', the book went flying as she hastened across the saloon, arms outstretched.

'You came,' she said. 'I am so pleased. Mama, here is Kitty at last. And see, she has brought Ann with her.'

All was then celebration and confusion, but after tears had been wept and eyes dried, the three young ladies were able to talk aside at the worktable whilst the older ladies entertained Mrs Bowman's young namesake.

'Have you thought about my offer?' asked Verity. 'Will you come back to Newmarket with us?'

'I would like nothing more, but I cannot. I cannot even leave Ann with you for safekeeping yet, not without reason. He is waiting for us now. He does not come into this part of town himself — I have learnt never to ask the reason for any of his actions — but he knows where we are. I have told him of Papa's death and your legacy. Now I will say that through Mama's kind offices, I hope to make connections for Ann which will be useful, the same way your godmother paid for you to go to school with Julia.'

'Will that be enough?'

'I hope so. He has unpleasant acquaintances. I would have Ann safely away before they take an interest in her.' Kitty looked from Verity to Julia, both of whom were regarding her with horror. 'I apologise if I distress you. Seven years ago I would have been the same. Life is different outside your drawing rooms and railed squares. It is hard and sometimes brutal, so we women shut it out and define our lives as normal. We focus on small triumphs like fashioning a fire out of gleanings from the coalman's yard. We count as a victory the swapping of a ribbon for enough coin for a beef shin bone to give body to the week's broth. It is a snatching of moments to create a happiness. And Simon is not always out of temper. He can be charming and complaisant so long as he is not crossed.'

Verity swallowed. 'What if he is?'

Kitty's mouth set into a line. 'He thinks he has me, therefore he makes sure to remind me that it is in my own interest to keep him comfortable. It is not what I want, nor what I expected when I went away with him, but . . . one adapts. When I judge it safe, I will escape to Newmarket, but I can never return to the girl I was after the things I have done and seen.' She met their eyes with the new, hard impatience Verity had noticed before. 'My fate is no different to that of many women who are sold off to older husbands for what their fathers can get. There may be a difference in scale, but we are all counters in a game.'

Verity assimilated this. 'What if . . . what if it were *our* game?'

'Our game? How could it be? How would we live? I could sell my own services for a competence, but there are laws against bawdy houses. Fines and hard labour if you're convicted of procuring for others.'

Verity shook her head slowly. 'I told you of my hopes for Furze House as a home for Mama and me. Charles thinks it too large for two women to rattle around in, too large even for three women and a child. But treating it as a house of safety away from London, where we let rooms to respectable ladies to ply whatever trade they choose, whether it be cooking or making bonnets or fashioning fans

— that would be a far more rational enterprise. We could hold card evenings or soirees now and again where gentlemen might come during the race meetings. Cards and music and light conversation is not procuring, is it?' Her mind threw up another possibility. 'And then, and once our little parties become known, it would give those gentlemen of Charles's acquaintance that he isn't overly anxious to be seen meeting a perfectly legitimate place to brush against each other.'

'In Newmarket,' mused Kitty. 'Up towards the racecourse? It has merit. That is the one place where such an arrangement might succeed. There would be several of us then? Like a boarding house, but one where we work together? I begin to like this scheme, Verity.'

'Molly Turner was saying she wished to get her mother and her children out of London. A laundry and repair facility in the yard would help make Furze House self-sustaining, would it not? You must know of other women who might be glad to swap the city for a country town. And the beauty of it is that to all intents and purposes, it would be a perfectly respectable dwelling.'

★   ★   ★

Julia and Verity walked with Kitty when she left. 'How far may we go with you?' asked Verity.

'To the bottom of Bond Street will be safe. If Simon is waiting along Piccadilly and happens to glimpse you returning, I can say you had purchases to make.'

'I do not want to let you leave. I wish you would stay.'

A yearning look crossed Kitty's face, instantly beaten back. 'So do I now. These last seven years have been so hard I had almost forgotten my early life still existed somewhere. So much softness, and love, and refinement. To have it so close . . . Do not tempt me, Verity. Not until we have made secure arrangements. If I left Simon now, I would fear for Ann's life with my every breath. I hope her new ribbons and the doll from Mama will prove to him that she is loved and of value as she is.'

Verity looked fondly down at her niece, and caught her exchanging a tiny wave with a street urchin who immediately took off down the road. She felt a pang of distress. There were always patched and ragged children around in London. Would that she could feed and clothe them all.

Where Bond Street became Piccadilly, Verity kissed her sister and picked up Ann to hug her. 'Goodbye, sweeting. I will see you again soon. Your grandmama is looking forward to you spending the whole day with us. Goodbye, Kitty, you will let me know when?'

'I will. Dearest Verity, thank you for still being your lovely stubborn self.' She took her daughter's hand and they walked resolutely away.

Verity turned to where Julia was tactfully studying a display of bonnets in a shop window. 'She is so much changed,' she said, struggling to keep her tears at bay.

'Still beautiful though,' said Julia. 'And her husband *was* waiting. You can see in the window . . . ' Her voice changed. 'Verity, don't turn around. Look here quickly. *Is* that her husband? Is that Captain Eastwick?'

Verity gazed blurrily at the reflected street. 'Yes, that is him. He didn't trust her at all, did he?'

'I begin to think she should not trust *him*,' said Julia with unusual acerbity. 'No wonder he does not normally come into our part of town. Verity, I was in daily contact with that gentleman not four months ago at the Cattsons' house party in Shropshire.'

'What? How?' Verity looked at her friend in shock. 'Why would he go to a house party and not take Kitty?'

Julia took a deep breath. 'Because at the time he was calling himself Mr

North and propositioning Mary Cattson. He was the gentleman her parents paid off.'

'Good God, can it be possible? Kitty said he often goes out of town and returns a few weeks later with money in his pocket. It that how he obtains it? By . . . by preying on the susceptibilities of young women? I cannot credit such a base thing.' But she realised she could believe it. As soon as he'd walked into the room at Henrietta Street, she'd felt his dominance and had remembered how he'd always liked to be the centre of attention. He had charmed Kitty in very short order seven years ago for no other reason than that he could. The only difference then had been that he'd married the object of his pursuit instead of being bought off. 'This is monstrous,' she said, feeling ill. 'To play with a woman's heart *knowing* that he is married and will never make good on his promises. It is despicable.' She turned, hurrying Julia back to the house. 'I must write a note to Charles that you may tell him the way of it yourself. The footman must go to his chambers if he is not at home.'

'Will Charles come just for that?'

'Oh yes. Do you not know your brother is a crusader? It is one of the things I admire him for. I daresay he will be knocking on the door as soon as he has read the letter.' Verity managed a smile. 'Your mama will think he has lost all his money, so often as he is turning up to dine in Grosvenor Street.'

Julia didn't smile. 'I have remembered something else,' she said. She met Verity's eyes, looking as if her stomach too had turned. 'On the morning Mr North left, one of the maids was found to have disappeared. She was a simple girl, but good-natured and trusting. What if she went with him? And if she did, where is she now?'

* * *

Charles listened to what Verity and Julia had to say, his intent, intelligent face

212

growing grimmer with each sentence.

'He is a blackguard. A man who preys on ladies' hearts to bolster his own sense of self and to feed his gaming habit. What if there are no young heiresses? It worries me that when in difficulties he may hold people's lives as cheaply as he does their emotions.'

'He did not hurt Mary Cattson physically, Charles,' said Julia. Further up the table, Mrs Congreve tutted to hear her daughter even speak of such possibilities.

'No, but he frequents a lawless milieu and Mrs Eastwick intimated he is dangerous. If he thinks he is likely to be unmasked, there is no telling what form his self-preservation might take. I would have you back in Newmarket, Verity, and Julia with you. He knows of you both now. He may think there are pickings to be had here.'

'Not without Kitty,' said Verity. 'I won't leave her with him.'

'Not before I have set Peter Crisp's feet on a straighter path,' said Julia. 'It may not seem much to you, brother, but I promised Sukie.'

'Not before I have Ann,' said Mrs Bowman, entering the conversation, an unfamiliar martial light in her eye. 'Kitty is my stepdaughter and not of my blood, but I was her mother as soon as ever I set eyes on her, and I will not fail her child. Would that I had had the strength of will to prevent her running away seven years ago.'

Charles threw up his hands. 'Lord preserve me from an army of women,' he said. 'Where is my father when I need him?'

'At the house, dear,' said Mrs Congreve helpfully.

'Thank you, Mama. Very well, if we can prevail on Mrs Eastwick and her daughter to grant you the pleasure of their company on a visit, will you all return to Kennet End until I can arrange for you to take up the lease of Furze House?'

'By the time we have persuaded Kitty to come with us, you will have arranged the lease three times over,' said Verity. 'She is near as obstinate as me.'

'Surely she will come when she hears about Mary Cattson,' said Julia.

'That is not the problem,' said Verity. 'She does not love Captain Eastwick any more or feel any loyalty to him. She is afraid of what he might do. By her account, he likes having power over people.'

'That is interesting,' remarked Mrs Bowman. 'The first time he came into Suffolk, we were all very pleased with his engaging address and pleasant manners. Even Mr Bowman was not against him. But a sennight later he came back from where they had been shooting, violent with rage. He said Captain Eastwick was an insufferable snake.'

Verity looked at her mother, startled. 'I do not remember that, Mama.'

Her mother frowned. 'I am trying to recall the details. I daresay you were not by. He moderated his anger quite soon, but held on to his dislike for the man,

215

and then announced Kitty was to marry Mr Prout.'

'I remember *that*,' said Verity. 'Kitty was so angry. She said she wouldn't and no one could make her.'

'And she did not. She eloped with Captain Eastwick.'

'But Mr Bowman did not pursue her,' said Charles. There was a thoughtful cast to his voice that made Verity look quickly at him.

He sees something, she thought, and a strange thrill ran through her. 'Charles? May we help?'

He sighed ruefully. 'This is my words coming back to haunt me. I was saying to Fitz only yesterday that you ladies are better at chasing out domestic details than any of my agents put together. I believe you *can* help in one respect, but I do not like it. What we require in order that your sister may be safe from Captain Eastwick is proof of his misleading these women. Is Miss Cattson in town, Julia? Can you enquire as to whether the maid ever returned? I could also bear to know how much her father paid 'Mr North', but I doubt you can find that out in conversation.'

'I can try,' said Julia.

'Please do. Is your sister to call again, Verity? Can you ask how much money her husband came home with from Shropshire? If indeed he told her he was going to Shropshire.'

'She may not know.'

'Meanwhile, I shall call on Bowman's attorney as Mr Tweedie suggested and attempt to extract a sum of money from him in recompense for Mrs Bowman giving up all claim to the dower house.'

'You are persuaded I am spending my time rationally, then?' Verity could not resist twinkling at him.

'If it is the only way to get you back to Newmarket, yes I am. I will, however, still need some sort of written record once you are home again in order to satisfy the Harringtons.'

'You are a prince amongst attorneys,

Charles. We should keep it to ourselves, though. I suggested Kitty tell her husband that the legacy conditions were why you were with me so much. Perhaps I should go with you to your chambers again to prove it, should anyone be watching.'

Charles smiled down at her. 'Once more, then. I will call on Monday morning and you may accompany me to your father's man. John's man, as he is now.'

'Thank you. And thank you for being concerned, but you should not worry about us working in our own way to find Captain Eastwick out. He is preying on our friends, doing it ruthlessly for his own gain, not caring that he breaks hearts and reputations. It could be any of us. In this, I think, we are all sisters.'

Beside her, Julia nodded emphatically.

Charles sighed. 'So I am learning.'

*　*　*

Sunday. Charles lay in bed, listening to the small sounds of Hicks moving about in the next room. The Albany Buildings were quiet. A day of rest. This time last week he had been in Suffolk, preparing for a leisurely breakfast with Verity and her mother. After church, they'd driven into Newmarket where they'd looked over Furze House by the simple expedient of Verity knocking on the door of the gardener's cottage, handing across a pot of honey from her brother's hives and obtaining the key. He felt his lips curve into a smile. She was exasperating and unstoppable and intelligent and completely adorable. Later they had dined with Adam and Jenny Prettyman, discussed local matters with Alex and Caro Rothwell and it had all been very pleasant. It reinforced his belief that *that* was the life Verity was designed for, and it was one he could not afford to give her.

He knew, beyond all shadow of a doubt, that he should stay as far away from her as possible. This was presumably why, when Hicks came in with shaving water and warm towels, he asked him to lay out a coat suitable for church-going and told him he would be breakfasting in Grosvenor Street. It was only himself he was torturing. She thought of him as a brother — and would be back in Newmarket very soon. Time enough then to remember how pleasing she looked with her head bent over a list with her mother, or whispering with Julia, or to recall the candlelight playing over her face as she read aloud to the company, her voice investing even the dullest book with interest.

13

On Monday morning there was an air of purpose about the Grosvenor Street breakfast table. Julia and her mother were to call on the Cattsons, Verity was ready for a morning with Charles, her mother would finish the lists of what to take from the dower house to Furze House and what they would need to purchase.

'Are you sure you would not rather call at the Temple with me?' asked Verity.

'No, dear; there is much to do if we are to remove as soon as Charles can arrange it. I own I am looking forward to the change, even though I shall be sorry to leave London. I am very much enjoying this visit. Pray tell George I would be pleased to see him again whenever he is at leisure. I had not realised how shackled I had become.

One forgets how wide the world is, when one is powerless to do anything but accept a situation.'

'You could come with me and tell him yourself,' suggested Verity.

Her mother exchanged a glance with Mrs Congreve. 'I would not distract him for the world. It is better if Charles deals with this matter.'

Verity puzzled over her mother's statement as Bridget inserted her into her outer costume. Better? Better why? In what way?

The Bowman attorney was located in a different building to Mr Tweedie's chambers. Verity tucked her hand into Charles's arm and remarked that for all they were there on business, this felt very much like a tour.

Charles smiled down at her. 'I did not know you had ever been on a tour, Verity. I cannot believe your father approved of such things.'

'He didn't, and I have not, but the mistresses at school used to take stout boots and walking sticks and go off together on a tour every summer. They would sketch what they saw and write it up in great long journals to form part of our instruction the next year. I used to read the journals aloud every evening while the other girls worked on their needlepoint.'

'That sounds a far more pleasant method of education than my school-days. Did it give you a curiosity for travel? Should you like to see new places?'

'Very much. I have been struck by something Mama said, that she had not realised how constrained she had become. I have learnt so much this week, Charles. There is a great deal more to the world than my narrow circuit. I am ashamed I know so little of it.'

Was it her imagination, or did his smile twist before he looked away. 'Perhaps when you are married, you and your husband can take tours of your own.'

She shook her head. 'I am not going

to marry. I believe that is how the restriction happens, unless one has the good fortune to meet with a very superior kind of gentleman. Jenny and Adam Prettyman are happy together, as are Caroline and Alexander Rothwell, but it is clear Kitty does not like being wed, and Mama seems not to have held her marriage to Papa in any affection. I shall be far better entertained keeping to the single state, going about as I like, and sharing Furze House with Kitty and the women she knows. Women who are not ashamed to work, but who fear men and the strength they carry with them. Women who need a refuge and a place of their own.'

'You cannot house them all, Verity.'

'That is no reason not to try.'

* * *

Mr Dryden's rooms were more cramped than Mr Tweedie's, and there was only one clerk in the outer office to the three that Charles and his partner kept busy. This accorded exactly with how Verity would have expected her father to do business.

Mr Dryden glanced at her disapprovingly. Realising Charles would be able to bargain far more persuasively without her presence, Verity bestowed a charming smile on the company and settled herself on a hard chair by the wall to wait.

Mr Dryden huffed, called for the papers relating to Mrs Bowman's jointure, then slammed the door into the inner sanctum behind himself and Charles. The clerk timidly asked Verity if she might move so he could lift the papers down from the shelf above her head.

'Certainly,' said Verity. 'It was not my intention to be in your way. May I assist in holding anything?'

'Thank you, miss. Such a lot of clients we have. The Bowman papers are those in the purple ribbon at the bottom of the pile. If you could just hold these, please, while I get them down . . .'

Verity balanced a tottering stack of papers, then passed them back one at a time once the required bundle had been retrieved. The Bowman papers proved to be an unwieldy accumulation of packets and when the clerk tried to extract the particular set required, the ribbon around them was found to be knotted.

'I need Mr Johnson's deeds,' ordered another attorney, striding through the door and glaring at the clerk. 'Now.'

'Certainly Mr Dent. I'll just — '

Verity stood up. 'Shall I undo the knot around our papers?' she offered. 'I have had a great deal of experience untangling snarls in ribbons and silks. There is a knack to it, I find.'

The harassed clerk accepted gratefully and Verity's fingers busied themselves with the purple ribbon. She located the key knot and gently teased it loose. The clerk and the other partner still had their backs turned while they looked for the missing deeds.

Curious, Verity riffled through the papers under the pretext of squaring them together more tidily. The top packets in the stack appeared to be mostly labelled 'boundaries' and 'fish-pond' and 'gifts to John', but halfway down was a slim package marked 'Papers relating to Catherine Margaret Bowman'. Verity didn't stop to think. She whipped it under her cloak. By the time the clerk had dealt with his other employer, she had redone the ribbon around the bundle with a perfect bow. 'There, that will make it easier for Mr Dryden to handle, will it not?' she said with a smile.

'My thanks, miss.' The man hurried it through Mr Dryden's door.

Some twenty minutes later, during which time Verity daren't look down for fear of seeing her cloak positively on fire with the purloined papers, Charles emerged with an air of satisfaction and escorted her back to his own chambers.

'It is possible a celebration is in order,' he said. 'Come through to my office while I jot down the main points of the discussion.'

This was fortunate. Verity immediately slid Kitty's papers from her cloak to the table. 'Oh, how foolish of me. I appear to have carried something off by mistake.'

Charles read the label and looked horrified.

'I hope it isn't something important,' she said mendaciously. 'That office was desperately untidy, was it not? Nothing like as well regulated as yours.'

'Verity . . . '

She looked at him, limpid-eyed.

One of the clerks appeared in the doorway with a letter. 'Just arrived, Mr Congreve. The gentleman's gone.'

Charles cleared his throat. 'Thank you. Do please have a seat, Miss Bowman.'

'Certainly.' She arranged herself sedately.

'Verity, where did you find these?'

'Halfway down that great bundle of papers. I did not see why John should have this package when it quite clearly pertains to Kitty.'

There was so much exasperation in his gaze that Verity almost quailed before it. 'Did you learn nothing at Bow Street? Does the term 'theft' hold so little meaning for you?'

'Fiddle. The place was in such a muddle, they will never miss it. And if they do, and if they happen to remember I was in the outer room — which they won't, for I am sure Mr Dryden looked through me as if I wasn't there — I have an excellent attorney.'

'One day, Verity, I will not be there to save you. Think on that the next time you have one of your impulses.' Nevertheless, he unfolded the sheets and read them through. He frowned and glanced over them again.

'Well?' asked Verity, unable to keep silent any longer.

'It is very puzzling. One sheet is a few lines signed by a Reverend Good recording the marriage between Captain Simon Eastwick and Miss

Catherine Margaret Bowman.'

'That does not sound puzzling.'

'The next sheet is an agreement stating that as Catherine has not made a suitable marriage as was stipulated in Mr Bowman's first wife's settlement, her half of the six thousand pounds from the late Mrs Bowman shall now be made over to her brother John on *his* making a suitable marriage, or on his majority, whichever is the sooner. In other words, he gets the whole settlement.'

'Oh, isn't that just like Papa. Everything was always for John. Always. Why do you look so perplexed? I assure you he would have given John the moon if he could.'

Charles tapped the documents softly. 'What puzzles me is how your father knew.'

'The whole of Kennet End knew Kitty and Mr Eastwick had eloped within an hour of the maid finding her note.'

'I am not disputing that, but how did

your father come by Kitty's marriage lines? She ran away. Her letters to your mother were never received, and in any case, this is hardly a thing she would have sent. How, then, is this document with his official papers? You said he did not go after her himself, or put any measures in place to find her.'

'He didn't. It was as if she ceased to exist as soon as she had left Kennet End. How strange. I shall ask when next I see her. Is there anything else in the packet?'

Charles lifted a slip of paper. 'A memorandum recording that the final five hundred pounds had been paid as agreed.'

'Five hundred pounds? To who? By who?'

'I do not know. It is unsigned and undated.'

'Perhaps it was caught up in Kitty's papers by mistake. It sounds like one of Papa's transactions.'

'Perhaps so. I would still like to know about the marriage lines. It also occurs to me that your sister was surely under age when she eloped. They would not have had permission for the marriage. I will take you back to Grosvenor Street, and then I think I may have to find this Reverend Good and put a few questions to him.'

'May I not come with you?'

'You may not. One meander through the less salubrious parts of the city is quite sufficient. I will call tomorrow and tell you my findings.'

★ ★ ★

As riddles went, it was an unsatisfactory one. Reverend Good had breathed his last several years previously. When Charles asked if there might be a note in the church ledger expressing any doubts or anything out of the ordinary about the marriage, the present incumbent said frankly that weddings weren't so common amongst his parishioners that any priest hereabouts was going to go asking for proof every time a bride assured him she was twenty-one.

Charles nodded his thanks and gave the man a couple of shillings for the poor relief.

The rector accepted the money cheerfully. 'I won't put it in the box. No sense tempting the congregation when it'll do more good in my housekeeper's soup cauldron. At least then everyone gets a share.'

'You know best. What did your predecessor die of?'

'A cosh to the back of the head. All for the cross around his neck and the thruppence three-farthings in his pocket.' The vicar brought forth a workmanlike truncheon from under his robes and hefted it fondly. 'God works in mysterious ways, Mr Congreve, but so far He's not regretted calling me to this parish.'

★ ★ ★

'That's a line of enquiry going nowhere. What of Mary Cattson, Julia?'

His sister smiled like a cat with a bowl of cream. 'Mr North was invited to the house by Mary's brother. It seems the foolish boy had lost money at play but Mr North, being a capital sort, tore up the IOUs and said he would not profit by a run of ill luck. The only thing was, he now found himself a trifle embarrassed until his money came in at the end of the quarter, so could he perhaps defray his expenses by staying quietly in the country with Cattson for a couple of weeks? Mary's brother naturally agreed to this, and there you have it. I declare, was there ever a more idiotic pair?'

'Gulled, both of them. Did you discover how much was paid?'

'Mary was sheltered from all such sordid talk. But she did say Frank's losses were in the region of £400, so I daresay that was paid and more again.'

'You have done extremely well. Thank you.'

'I enjoyed it. Is there any future, do you suppose, in hiring oneself out as a female Bow Street Runner?'

'None,' replied Charles crushingly.

'That is a shame. What do we investigate next?'

'Nothing. I am for my chambers. You will no doubt prepare for whichever party you are attending this evening.'

'All this studying of the law has made you very cross, Charles. However, as we are invited to Mrs Stanhope's rout this evening, though where she is to find enough people at this time of year to warrant the name is a matter of considerable conjecture, I should perhaps look over my gowns.'

She drifted out of the room. Verity smiled at Charles. 'I neglected to thank you for battling Mr Dryden on Mama's behalf yesterday.'

He took her hand in his. 'Don't tell Julia, but I enjoyed it very much. The man is as prosy as your brother. I may drop by his rooms again to ensure he treats the matter with despatch.'

'Will you return Kitty's papers?'

He smiled down at her. 'The place

was in such disarray, they will never miss them.'

'Charles!'

'You are a terrible influence, Verity. Goodbye. I hope you do not find this evening too much of a crush.'

'Do you not attend?'

'I am rarely invited. Many people find themselves perplexed by the social anomalies inherent in entertaining a gentleman who is also a practising attorney.'

Verity looked disapproving. 'It does not seem to me in any way an odd thing to invite doctors or attorneys or bankers to the dinner table, but perhaps that is because I am used to country habits. It appears to be different in London, and not nearly so intelligent. Is it difficult for you balancing your profession with your friends?'

There were times when she was too perspicacious for comfort. Charles hurriedly dropped her hand and left the room in search of his hat and gloves. 'I have never thought so before.'

14

'Lieutenant Crisp, how nice. Have you been drilling diligently?'

The young officer blushed as Verity addressed him. 'Yes indeed, though it is not the same in England, with no enemy to outmanoeuvre. I had hopes we might be sent overseas again, but the word is our next posting is to Liverpool.'

'How disappointing. Liverpool is accounted a fine city though, is it not?'

'Oh yes, my home is in those parts, so I have been there many times. The posting is convenient in that respect, but I like the reduced leisure time when we are overseas.' He coloured faintly. 'I am not very skilled at cards or dice, Miss Bowman. I prefer to be doing than gaming.'

'I see. I am afraid I know little of the army. Can you perhaps volunteer for extra duties?'

His expression lightened. 'That is what Miss Congreve suggested. Thank you. I will ask my captain.'

They were interrupted by the lazy drawl of another officer, his red coat nudging between Verity and Lieutenant Crisp in a manner just stopping short of impertinence. 'What's this, Crisp? First Miss Congreve, now Miss Bowman. We can't have you monopolising all the ladies. I have barely spoken to either of them this evening.' He lifted Verity's fingers in what was presumably supposed to be a deferential manner and dropped a less-than-welcome kiss on them.

Verity stiffened in shock. Not only had Lieutenant Neville barely spoken to her this evening, he had barely spoken to her ever. She had not even realised he saw her as a presence in her own right. She jerked her hand free and moved slightly away. 'We were talking of Liverpool and the fine architecture. Do you know the port?'

'I can't say I do. London, now, I'm far more at home in. I could show you plenty of the sights here. Vauxhall Gardens, perhaps, or Ranelagh. Have you ever been to Ranelagh, Miss Bowman? I assure you it is an experience one does not soon forget.'

Verity might not be as conversant with London and its many attractions as Julia, but even had she only this minute heard of the pleasure gardens, the caress in Lieutenant Neville's voice told her what sort of experience she was likely to get there. 'I was taken as a child to see the fireworks. Excuse me, gentlemen, but my mother is beckoning.'

She whisked away, wiping her fingers on her skirt to rid herself of Lieutenant Neville's touch. If Julia had been putting up with similar veiled invitations, it was a wonder she did not spend all her time scrubbing her hands under the scullery pump.

As she skirted chattering groups, she asked herself what she was doing at parties such as this. She had found Kitty, which had been her primary object in coming to London. She was satisfied Julia was not about to make a fool of herself. Mama was happier and livelier that she had been for years. Charles seemed in a fair way to granting access to her legacy. All that was left was to persuade Kitty to return to Newmarket, which could not be accomplished at a rout party.

'Verity, dear,' said her mother, bright-eyed and animated. 'Let me introduce you to Mrs Pinkerton. Mrs Pinkerton has been telling me of her villa in Kensington. She has invited us to take tea there tomorrow. It sounds completely charming and there are several vacant houses nearby of the same type. I have been wondering if we might move to London rather than Furze House, so nice as it is to be with our friends here and for you to visit the attractions and mix in society more. What do you think, my dear?'

With an enormous effort of will, Verity prevented her horror at the idea from showing on her face. 'It is certainly an interesting idea, Mama.' She turned to the comfortable matron sitting next to her parent. 'I look forward to tomorrow's visit, Mrs Pinkerton. Have you resided in the area long?'

This was a disaster, she thought in despair, making her way to Julia after listening to a comprehensive recital of the villa's advantages. She was delighted Mama was taking an interest in life again, but Kitty would never come to Kensington. It was by far too close to her husband. Additionally, without Mama's allowance to combine with her own legacy, Verity could not afford Furze House. She wished Charles was here to talk to, even more so when she was thwarted in her intention of a *tête-à-tête* with Julia by the sight of the officers now forming part of her friend's circle. Instead she turned to compliment Miss Stanhope on the excellent arrangements. The easy words fell from her lips. Inside she was distraught.

Miss Stanhope beamed and chattered, clearly under the impression she had made a new friend. 'We are to have an impromptu hop,' she confided. 'I am sure everyone enjoys a dance. Everything is planned and Miss Green has practised the music. My mother is simply waiting on anyone particularly well-connected arriving, so they may be welcomed first.'

'Inspired,' murmured Verity, wondering if her hostesses knew the meaning of impromptu.

Miss Stanhope jiggled excitedly and gave a suppressed squeal. 'Oh, the officers are rolling back the carpet. Lieutenant Neville moves very well, does he not? One would think the effort nothing. He is coming over! He is going to ask me to dance, I know it. Oh, Miss Bowman, whatever shall I say? Our neighbour Mr Hollis was supposed to lead me out.'

'Then you should move swiftly to your mama as if you have noticed nothing. Come, I will go with you so as not to make it look singular.'

Miss Stanhope turned with evident reluctance as Verity linked her arm firmly in hers. 'But there is something about Lieutenant Neville that is quite delicious, don't you think?'

Verity managed not to retort that she should stay and have her heart broken and see how delicious she found it. Instead she conscientiously steered the impressionable young lady to the safety of her mother's machinations. *Now I can talk to Julia*, she thought, only to be frustrated once again, and this time most unpleasantly.

'What a noble guest,' purred Lieutenant Neville in her ear. 'Will you do me the honour of partnering me in the first dance?'

'I regret I must sit this out,' said Verity, cross that he had come up so very close behind her without invitation or encouragement. 'I have a headache and would no doubt stumble over my own feet.'

He smiled widely. 'Then I shall bear

you company. No one should suffer a headache alone.'

Verity's temper snapped. 'I should be very poor company and am better left alone. Pray do not let me prevent you from enjoying yourself.'

'So modest. So delightful. Come, Miss Bowman, confess. Is not the music setting those dainty toes a-twitch?'

She stared in disbelief, furious that he was persevering. She was on the point of telling him her feet were in fact a-twitch to administer a sharp kick, when her elbow was grasped from behind and she was borne towards the set then forming with a careless, 'My apologies, Miss Bowman; I was delayed. I trust you will forgive me.'

'Charles, you are a complete saviour,' she said in deep thankfulness as they took their places. 'I have never been gladder to see anyone. I am not even going to ask why you are here uninvited.'

'It would be of no use, for I scarcely

know myself. You are not the only one who has had a trying evening.'

★ ★ ★

Earlier that evening
'Well, Nick, what do you have for us?' said Fitz.

As Nicholas Dacre entered, Charles roused himself from his contemplation of Fitz's notes on the latest bruised and battered anonymous woman fished out of Limehouse Basin. They were meeting in his own rooms tonight — the Albany was populous enough that a watcher would find nothing unusual in the casual arrivals and departures of any number of gentlemen. He waved Nick towards the decanter.

'Good evening, gentlemen,' said Nick. 'Sad to say, I have nothing. Molly Turner was pleased to share a cosy supper with me in the upper room of an inn a little way from the theatres. We discussed a great many plays, I find my mind quite astonishingly expanded as regards the iniquities practised by malicious folk who like to defraud an honest woman out of an honest penny, but as soon as the word Flint crossed my lips not one scrap more could I get from her.'

'A rare failure.'

'Indeed. She has a refreshingly direct approach and was happy to talk or not as I wanted, but give away anything that might come back to hurt her or her kin she would not.'

'Did she say as much, Nick?'

'In those very words. Then finished her supper as pleasant as could be, tucked her money away and trotted off.'

Benedict Fitzgilbert drummed his fingers lightly on the table. 'More and more I believe this Flint to be our shadowy gentleman. He has got them all running scared. Not a single loose mouth. Just the odd word, dropped like a crumb from a table.'

Charles stirred. 'It speaks of money. Or power. He has to have a network.

Why do we not know his thugs at the very least?'

'Because if we so much as get a sniff of one, they're in the river next morning with their throat slit.'

'Just like these poor nameless women,' said Charles, touching Fitz's notes. 'Battered, abused, discarded.'

'Indeed,' said Fitz soberly. 'We can only keep trying. I had hopes of your Molly Turner, Charles, but it was not to be. Speaking of obstinate females, what progress are you making on the lesser matter of the charming Captain Eastwick?'

Charles gestured helplessly. 'It may be a lesser matter to you, but it is not to Kitty Eastwick. Hers is a hard-won caution. She says she married him with her eyes open, but she did not. How could she? She was born and brought up a gentleman's daughter. She could not have known what her life would be with Eastwick. He is a charismatic predator, a bully, a gamester and appears entirely without morals.'

Nick raised an eyebrow. 'That's quite a list. You haven't thought he may be Flint?'

Charles shook his head. 'His life is too open. I had a man watching him until he felt himself to be observed in turn. Simon Eastwick is bad through and through, but I don't get the sense of a great criminal mind at work. He strives to be the lord of his village pond, not of the whole ocean.'

Fitz nodded. 'What is your next move?'

'I am open to suggestions. Julia already has proof of his deceit where one young lady is concerned. Sadly, it is not sufficient to bring him to trial without compromising the family and exposing the young woman to scandal and shame. I would prefer *not* to create a scandal. Revealing his card-sharping seems a more promising line.'

Nicholas sipped his wine. 'It maybe an irregular source of knowledge, but your womenfolk are certainly getting results, Charles. Look how quickly they found out about the Pool when they put their information together.'

'Irregular is right. They do not know when to stop. I would have both Verity and Julia safely out of town, but they will not leave without Mrs Eastwick and she is too scared to move. I am expediting the matter of Furze House as fast as possible.'

Fitz regarded him thoughtfully. 'Nick's levity has a grain of truth. Ladies go where we cannot. They trust each other where they do not trust us. I have noticed it with my sister. A few careful female conversations now and again could save us a deal of time.'

Charles beat down a spurt of irrational rage and forced himself to examine the idea coolly. He came to the reluctant conclusion that Fitz might be right. 'It is a possibility,' he admitted, 'but I would still have them away from London. There may yet be hope for a word from Molly. Verity's latest plan is to invite her to Newmarket also and to turn the rear of Furze House into a laundry to help with finances.' He braced himself for the inevitable ribald comments.

'A laundry?' said Nick, with a shout of laughter. 'Is that what those houses are called these days?'

Charles drained his glass. 'She insists it will be respectable. She says they will entertain morning callers and hold card evenings and sewing afternoons for their friends and go about their normal daily business.' He paused, then added unwillingly, 'She also suggests that if Furze House is *not* thought entirely respectable, then it would be the perfect location for the Pool to meet or exchange reports when out of town, because any curious outsiders will imagine us gentleman are otherwise engaged. I declare I will hang for the minx. She should not even know of these things. She will be tarnished by association if such a rumour gets abroad. Now do you see why I wish to remove her from town and settle her respectably?'

The other two men exchanged a considering look.

'I understand your objections regarding Miss Bowman's reputation, but it is not necessarily a *bad* plan to have a house in Newmarket where we could meet,' said Nick cautiously. 'I certainly could have done with one last week. Arriving at the race meeting so late, I had a desperate time finding a room. I ended up in a truckle bed in the loft of the White Hart along with half-a-dozen of the worst topers in town. Don't hate me, Charles, but I did look over Furze House out of curiosity and was favourably impressed. Think man, Rothwell keeps horses with his brother-in-law. You have clients in Suffolk. I daresay Fitz visits the racecourse too.'

'I don't, but I have a sister who would be delighted to request my escort in order to search out any or all antiquities in the area. She would be as ready as the others to join your irregulars, though preferably *without* the taint of scandal. Newmarket is less than a day's journey from London. It seems a workable plan when we have large schemes to put together. If you require finance, it's yours.'

'You are both impossible,' said Charles shortly. He passed a hand across his forehead. 'Forgive me, gentlemen; I am appalling company today.'

Fitz rose. 'We are done in any case. I shall ensconce myself in a corner of White's and no one will know how long I have been there.'

'I will fence,' said Nicholas, lazily stretching. 'I'll give you time to get clear, Fitz.'

Fitz nodded and left.

'You know, Charles,' said Nick, 'I've seen you flatten a bully, I've seen you tie up a thief with one hand and I've seen you at the card table stripping a cheat of his winnings without breaking sweat. It is not like you to be out of sorts. Is it Miss Bowman?'

'Damn your eyes, Nick.'

'What is the objection?'

'There is no objection, because it will not happen. She is a gentleman's daughter. I am a working attorney with barely a pound to my name. If I am out of sorts, it is because I am concerned for her reputation.'

Nicholas tossed down the remains of his wine and sauntered towards the door. 'There are only two options when a woman gets to you. Love 'em or leave 'em.'

Charles rose with a growl, but his friend was gone, the door closing behind him. It was probably as well. Nick would certainly get the better of him if he followed him to the fencing salon. He'd get some fresh air and walk off his temper instead.

He'd covered a good mile before realising two things simultaneously. One, that he was walking his temper on, not off. And two, that he was within two streets of tonight's rout party. With a fatalistic shrug, he continued. If Julia was correct, the Stanhopes would be too desperate for company to turn away a Mr Congreve, even if he *was* an attorney by day and only a gentleman in the evenings.

The butler ushered him in without batting an eyelid. Already regretting his impulse, Charles walked into an over-heated saloon to the unmistakable strains of a governess playing the introduction to a country dance on the piano. It was, he thought cynically, one way of hanging on to guests for as long as possible. He looked around for Verity — and saw a scene across the room that drove everything else from his mind. An officer was lifting Verity's hand to his lips in a manner exactly calculated to make any other red-blooded gentleman in the room want to kick him clear across the continent into the nearest war.

Verity drew back. The officer took a step forward.

Rage bubbled in Charles's veins. He strode across the room, scooping up Verity with a curt apology, and marched her towards the nearest set.

'Charles, you are a complete saviour,' said Verity. 'I have never been gladder to see anyone. I am not even going to ask why you are here uninvited.'

'It would be of no use, for I scarcely know myself. You are not the only one who has had a trying evening.'

'I am sorry about that, but glad of the result, for if you had not arrived precisely then, I should have been banned from polite society for ever.'

'If he follows us, we might both be,' growled Charles. 'Why were you encouraging him?'

'I was not encouraging him!' Verity shook herself free. 'He is most unpleasant. What are you doing here, Charles?'

He replaced her hand on his arm. 'Rescuing you. Why was he being so gallant?'

Verity's fingers shook a little. 'I do not know. From being happily ignorant of my existence, he is now crowding me beyond anything comfortable. Whatever the reason for the sudden change, I do not like it.'

'He is dead if he comes within ten feet of you,' promised Charles.

'That would certainly add an *éclat* to Mrs Stanhope's rout party. I'm sorry, Charles, as you say, it has been a very vexing evening. And now I must smile and dance when I have never felt less inclined.'

Charles was assailed by guilt. 'I forgot you are in mourning. I should not have acted so precipitously. Shall I escort you home instead?'

'I daresay you will be glad to after this set. I do not at all mind dancing with you, Charles, but I am too cross to concentrate on the steps. Your feet will be black and blue.' Showing her true mettle, she then smiled prettily, stepped back and curtsied as the piano gave the signal.

Indignant as she was, angry as *he* was, there was nevertheless much pleasure in partnering Verity. She crossed and re-crossed the first figure with a grace that brought forth the best from the others in their set. The touch of her fingers on his when they circled and turned was light and assured. Charles's wrath ebbed away, soothed by the music and the matching of their steps and the mathematical gratification of the pattern.

'Oh, that was marvellous,' said Miss Stanhope when the music stopped. There was a pink flush in her cheeks and her eyes shone. 'I have never danced it so well before.'

'You were wonderful,' said her partner.

Verity met Charles's eyes. 'One task complete,' she murmured. 'Do you think we might sit out now?'

'I believe so. What has happened to discompose you, Verity?'

'Lieutenant Neville being irksome, a sense that I am wasting time, Mama . . . ' Someone bumped her shoulder and she glanced around with exasperation. 'Why is there nowhere one can have a private conversation?'

'If there were, the rout would be

deemed a disaster. Do you wish to leave?'

'That would be heavenly,' said Verity. 'Can it be done without giving offence?'

'Certainly. You are overset with the high quality of the entertainment.'

'How appallingly poor-spirited. Let us inform Mama and Godmama, then congratulate Mrs Stanhope on her party and take our leave.'

Charles had to bite his cheek as Verity assured her mother she would be fine by the morning and told her on no account to cut short her own delightful evening. She shook her hostess's hand, whispered something to Julia as she passed and they waited in the hallway until her wrap might be found.

Charles was just settling it around her shoulders and asking with a frown why she had not brought her Norwich shawl as better proof against the night air rather than this thin one, when he heard Lieutenant Neville's unmistakable drawl from the other room. By the wintry look in Verity's eyes, she could hear him too.

'It is easy to see how the wind blows in that quarter. Evidently the attorney thinks to get his hands on the money.'

'Home ground, Neville,' said another of the officers. 'You can't deny it's an advantage.'

'The thrill of the chase is in the challenge. Anyone care for a wager?'

15

Fury filled Verity. *That* was why Lieutenant Neville had been so persistent. He was after her legacy. Her fists bunched. Why was it not permissible for ladies to knock down unwelcome suitors in other people's drawing rooms?

Looking up, she saw a similar murderous rage in Charles's eyes. The shock brought her back to her senses. If Charles took action it would have far worse consequences than if she did. She could return to Newmarket to avoid a scandal. He would have his livelihood affected if he started a brawl.

'Lieutenant Crisp should apply for a transfer,' she said, with as much boredom as she could summon. 'His fellow officers seem appallingly vulgar.' When Charles didn't move, she shook his arm. 'May we leave?'

Inside the hackney carriage, she leaned back against the squabs, infinitely more at ease than she had been in the house. 'This is better. I could barely think in that crowd. Julia will be sadly disappointed in me, but I do not believe I am cut out for a vigorous social whirl. I wonder she never tires of the constant round herself.'

Charles remained silent.

He is hurt and angry, and no wonder. 'Do you object if I rest against you? Irritation is very fatiguing.'

'Are you sure you trust me?' he said bitterly.

'Dearest Charles, don't be so ridiculous,' she said, tucking her arm inside his. 'I would trust you with my life.'

He sighed and returned from whichever stormy paths he had been striding. 'I apologise. I offer you my escort and then pay you no heed. What else has upset you tonight that you wished to tell me? You should not curl up like this, Verity; it is most improper.'

Good. She had broken through his

silence. 'Fudge. Who is to see us? Oh Charles, the most frustrating occurrence. Just as we have everything settled, Mama has decided she would like to live in Kensington! In a villa.'

'Kensington?' Charles sounded as horrified as she had been. 'That would be a disaster.'

'So I think too. Kitty will never come to us in Kensington.'

Silence. 'No,' said Charles, a heartbeat too late. 'It is too close to her husband. She and the child would not be safe.'

That had not been the first thought in his mind. Verity felt as if she had been walking in comfortable darkness and missed a step. She twisted to look up at him. 'Why else would Kensington be a disaster?'

It was dim in the carriage and his head was close to hers. The glow of a lamp as they passed showed panic and helplessness and something else, hurriedly suppressed, in his eyes.

In that split second, hanging in time,

everything changed. A piercing content-ment awoke in her. 'Oh,' she said, and her heart banged. Charles. Of course.

'Verity, I . . . '

Her lips were still parted. She raised them to his at the exact instant the horses slowed.

'Exquisite timing, Charles, as ever,' he muttered, and opened the door ready to hand her out.

★ ★ ★

The moment was gone. Charles was Charles again, the elder brother John had never been. Verity took a moment in the hallway to shake out her skirts and glance at her flushed face in the glass. How foolish of her. He was being absolutely correct. She should follow his example.

They were friends, that was all. It wasn't as if she was ever going to marry, not now she didn't have to. Or did she? If Mama wanted to live in Kensington, Furze House would be impossible. Without their shared income, Verity's dream of being able to help her sister and those other women would vanish.

Charles had already bespoken tea and was waiting for her to precede him into the salon. She brushed past, caught the warmth of his body and the faint scent of his cologne and was instantly back in the carriage. She was astounded at the enormous jolt of awareness. It was perfectly obvious to her that he felt it too.

'Charles,' she said. 'If you sit anywhere except next to me on this sofa, I may never speak to you again.'

His lips curved into a reluctant smile as he dropped into the armchair.

'Beast.'

'Minx,' he replied. 'Verity, it will not do. I am an attorney. Your attorney.'

That was so much nonsense she could hardly believe he was saying it. She moved up to the corner of the sofa nearest his chair. 'Is that why you do not wish me to live in Kensington?'

'It would be a disaster,' he repeated.

She held his gaze. 'Why did you come to the Stanhope rout party tonight?'

'Truth to tell, I hardly know.'

Tenderness swelled her heart. The frustrations of the evening suddenly seemed immaterial. '*You will know when it is right,*' Jenny had told her, and she did. Why had she never realised before? 'I do not think we should deal so very badly together,' she said softly.

He gave a sudden laugh. 'It would be an adventure of the highest order, but it cannot happen. I work for a living. You have plans and ambitions. You deserve more than a man who would need your own money to support you.' He looked down and realised she was holding his hands. 'Stop it, Verity,' he said, disengaging them. 'I have my pride. May we put the subject away and discuss the problem of your mother and your sister and *my* sister?'

Verity's heart lifted because Charles was *not* simply Charles and there was nothing elder-brotherly about the way he was denying the attraction. All her disappointment and setbacks and helplessness were now merely obstacles to be surmounted. It did not occur to her not to continue. For one thing, the idea of kissing him had entered her head and it was going to be really rather difficult to get it out.

'By all means,' she said. 'To begin with, Julia is in no danger. She is saving Lieutenant Crisp from himself as a favour to his sister. She believes Lieutenant Neville is trying to corrupt him. It does seem so, but I do not know why he should, unless it is just idle mischief. His actions tonight show how irresponsible he is.' She frowned, her words trailing off.

'What is the matter?'

'How did Lieutenant Neville know of Uncle James's legacy?'

Charles spread his hands. 'You ask that with Julia's example daily before you? Gossip disseminates.'

'The legacy is not yet common

currency. Lieutenant Neville did not consider me of any value at the gallery. Now he does. Peter Crisp told Julia that Neville owes him money. Perhaps he thinks to borrow it from me?'

'Gentlemen do not borrow from ladies. Depend on it, the word will have come from Julia. Her heart is in the right place, but her tongue is never still.'

'I will ask her. Meanwhile, what are we to do about Mama?'

'You know her better than I. Is she much given to these impulses?'

'I have never known her do such a thing before, but she has been different since we came to London, particularly since Mr Tweedie was here. She must have been truly crushed before, and is learning how to breathe again. I would not set her back, but I do not wish to live here.'

'I own I cannot picture you in a villa in Kensington, but would it be so hard?'

There was genuine curiosity in

Charles's voice. Verity responded with a serious answer. 'I think it would. Uncle James need not have worried about my frivolity. I cannot take part in the social round any more, Charles, not now I have seen behind the facade. I want to help. I want Furze House for Kitty and Molly and their friends. If we can sustain it, then I want to open up another house after that. You have wrought better than you knew. How can I give myself to careless enjoyment when children are transported for stealing a handkerchief?'

'I did not mean to cut up your peace.' He hesitated. 'Things will change, Verity. There is a reform movement in the House. Men do care. Your friend Caroline's husband is amongst them.'

'It will not be changed next week though, or next month.'

'Nor even next year, but I believe it is coming. Verity, regarding Furze House — I should not say this but my pool of associates consider a neutral, respectable house in Newmarket would be an asset to our resources when we wish to meet. Yes, you may crow over me if you must. I have suffered so much mortification today that a little more will make no difference. If Mrs Bowman is fixed on staying here in London, there will still be finance forthcoming for you to take Furze House.'

Verity's eyes shone. 'Charles, how splendid. Is this Lord Fitzgilbert's doing? Julia says he is remarkably rich. How may I live there though? I am not yet twenty-one.'

'Your sister is twenty-five. A married woman may easily chaperone her sister, even if she has left the protection of her husband.' He turned his head, listening, and then stood up. 'Is that the carriage? I had best go. I will apprise Mr Tweedie of your mother's notion. It may well be he will persuade her to move back to Newmarket. I have never yet known him choose a bold option over a safe one.'

Verity jumped up. 'Thank you, Charles.' She reached up on tiptoe to kiss his cheek, but he turned his head back at that moment so she caught the side of his mouth instead.

There was a second of absolute stillness between them. Her heart thudded so loudly she confused it with the noise of the street door opening. Charles was quicker. He dropped his hand from her arm where *surely* he had been going to take proper hold of her, and was straightening his cravat in the mirror as his mother bustled into the room.

'Still here, Charles? There, Anne, I said he would not abandon poor Verity to her headache.'

'Indeed, it was very kind of him,' said Verity, disorientated by the normality that had swept into the salon along with the rustle of silk and the soft fluff of Julia's feathered muff.

'But I must take my leave now, Mama,' said Charles. He kissed his mother, saluted Mrs Bowman's hand

and just stopped short of lifting Verity's fingers to his lips as well.

Oh, Charles.

'I will inform you as soon as events move forward,' he said, and left.

'Which events?' asked Julia.

'Something about the terms of Uncle James's legacy. Have you mentioned it to anyone, Julia? Lieutenant Neville was tiresomely attentive this evening.'

'No, we have only told Lilith, and she would not spread it around. How intriguing. Is the good lieutenant short of money, do you suppose? Peter Crisp says he does a great deal of card playing, not always for low stakes.'

'There is nothing good about him that I can see. Why do you look troubled?'

A shadow came into her friend's eyes. 'The saddest thing. Peter told me one of their number — Lieutenant Oaks, I do not know if you recall him — shot himself two days ago. Did you not notice the black bands they were all wearing?'

'How very dreadful. The poor man's family.'

'I do not envy his superior officer. How do you tell a young woman with two small children that she is now a widow? Also that there is no money, because her husband gambled it away and took his own life rather than face up to his actions? It does not bear thinking of. I am out of sorts, Verity. I should have come home when you did. I believe I will go to bed.'

'I too,' said Verity. But it was a long time before she slept.

★   ★   ★

'Were you wishful of a hackney, miss?'

Verity came out of her thoughts and looked up at the hackney carriage that had moved forward as she and Julia descended the steps of the house. 'Oh, is it you, Mr Grimes? How very fortunate. Yes please, and how is your horse today?'

'Verity,' said Julia, enchanted. 'You

'know the most delicious people.'

'This is Mr Grimes, Julia, who has driven me on a couple of occasions.'

'Pleased to meet you. I've a message for you, miss. From Molly. She says yes and gladly to your proposition, what was passed on by your sister. Just send her word and the address and she'll pack 'em all up and make her way there.'

'Oh, that's splendid. Molly Turner and her family are to come to Furze House, Julia.'

Fred Grimes had not yet finished. 'And she has a bit of information your gentleman friend might be interested in if she's right in her thinking, but it didn't come from her.'

'Didn't come from . . . Oh, I understand. What is it, please?'

'He's to go to the Bridewell and ask for Susan Norris.'

'Susan Norris. Thank you. I will send him a note directly. I suppose the Bridewell is not a place my friend and I could visit, is it?'

Julia let out a shriek. Apparently not, then.

'Well,' said Fred Grimes doubtfully, 'ladies *do* go around it sometimes, on a charitable visit like, or just to view the poor desperate souls, but it would have to be Mr Congreve ask the questions.'

'You know him?' asked Verity, surprised.

'We all know the ones who help poor folk, miss.'

'Very well, thank you for the message that I have no recollection of you giving me, and I will send Charles a note as soon as we return. Which drapers have I not yet visited, Mr Grimes? Suitable for a large house, but not with a large budget?'

'I know the very place, miss. This large house, is it in the country?'

'Yes. It is at Newmarket. It is where Molly was referring to.'

'Would there be a place in the stable for an old horse and driver? One who might do local deliveries if there was any call for it? There's only me and the horse left now, and it's powerful bad for me and the old girl here, isn't it, lass?' He patted the horse's flank.

'There is stabling, and a room over it,' said Verity. 'That would be wonderful. Might you bring Molly and her mother and the children to save expense? It's sixty miles.'

'I was thinking of it, miss. Or follow on after with her bits and pieces. We could take it slow. What's a sennight or two on the road with new life ahead? God bless you, miss.'

'This house of yours is going to be extraordinary,' said Julia as they set off. 'I am almost tempted to invent a scandal so I must rusticate with you.'

'You can come for a visit without being embroiled in a scandal first,' pointed out Verity. 'I am more concerned with getting Kitty there without her husband suspecting.'

Julia looked thoughtful. 'You will need to, for your mama will never consent to you living there without her otherwise.'

'I am still in hopes she will give up this Kensington scheme.'

'She did not seem to be giving it up when we went around the villa yesterday. She seemed enchanted by the whole idea.'

'I quite thought Mr Tweedie would say she cannot afford it instead of encouraging her,' said Verity gloomily. 'It is a nice house, but . . . '

'Too out of the way for me. I should never hear anything of any note. Why would Charles not come around it with us?'

Because he is avoiding me. 'Perhaps they cannot both be away from the chambers at the same time.' But that was nonsense, for they had come up to Newmarket together earlier this year to apprehend Jenny Prettyman's cousin. 'It would have done no good even if he had been there. Charles is as perplexed as I am about Mama.'

In truth, Verity was more than perplexed, she was dumbfounded at the change that had come over her mother this last week. It was as if she had never known her before. Her eyes were brighter, her bearing more cheerful and, only two days since she had first mooted the idea, she was full of optimism about living in Kensington.

'See, my dear, it is almost rural here, though but a short ride into town,' she had said happily yesterday. 'And neighbours so close, not like at Kennet End, where if we see anyone from one day to the next it is only John and Selina or Reverend Milsom.'

Verity wanted to tell her they would have nearer neighbours at Furze House, but she didn't know how to deal with Mama in this strange new mood. Was this her natural state? One her marriage had suppressed? It was plain Mr Tweedie found little difference in her to the Miss Harrington he had known twenty years before.

She was so confused. She would have to frame her note in such a way that Charles called to hear the substance of it. Things always seemed clearer after she had talked to him.

The hackney carriage slowed to a stop. Fred Grimes took the fare with thanks and asked if he should wait.

'That would be very kind, but we might be half an hour.'

'It's no matter to me. I've paid off what I borrowed for my poor wife's medicines, not that they did her any good in the end. I was determined to do it, even if it near crippled me. I'm just marking time now, if you take my meaning.'

They went into the warehouse. Julia linked arms with her friend. 'I daresay if you sat up beside him you would have his whole history by the time we were home.'

'Do not be superior, Julia. You know you do the same with the society people you meet. Think of Peter Crisp and tell me it isn't so.'

'People's lives are interesting.'

'So I think too. We are simply interested in different spheres.'

Necessary purchases made, Julia

sighed. 'I am so tired of not having any allowance left. I dearly wish I could afford a new bonnet. I will have to trim an old one afresh.'

Verity turned in the act of climbing back into the hackney carriage. 'Shall we go to one of the bazaars? It is very frivolous and not at all a rational use of our time, but I do think some pretty ribbon for my grey cambric would cheer it up. Pink, perhaps, or cherry? Respectful colours are depressing.'

Fred Grimes cleared his throat. 'Would the Soho Bazaar suit your purpose, miss?'

'The very place!' said Julia, brightening.

'Where is that, Mr Grimes?' asked Verity at the same time. 'I have not heard of it.'

'Opened last year, miss. It's for widows and daughters of soldiers to sell millinery and trimmings and suchlike. Mr Trotter, he only charges thruppence for a foot of counter, so all the women share the shop and can make their pieces at home and then sell them. Over a hundred of them there are.'

Verity beamed at him. 'What a splendid idea. Please do take us there. You see, Julia, this is the sort of aim I had in mind for Furze House. A place where everyone can work together. No one bears the whole burden.'

Soho Square itself was formed of well-proportioned houses, but there were so many carriages waiting that the hackney was obliged to stop some way away from the bazaar.

'Do not wait,' said Verity. 'It will take us a deal of time to go around.'

'I'll bide until I get another fare. If I'm not here when you come out, another hackney will be along.'

'Assuming we can afford one by then,' replied Verity. 'My friend has a tremendous eye for a bargain, never more so than when she is laying out someone else's money.'

Despite the accuracy of this prophesy, there remained a few coins in Verity's purse when they emerged. This was largely, as she pointed out, because she had refused to lend her friend enough for an embroidered reticule in forget-me-not blue silk the exact colour of Julia's eyes when she knew perfectly well Julia had another two of that same shade at home. Her friend replied that they were not at all the same blue and Verity was hard-hearted indeed not to have indulged her.

Walking nearly two sides of the square in quest of Mr Grimes, with their arms full of parcels and their attention on the argument, they did not see a gentleman emerge from a house and descend the steps. As parcels flew in all directions and Julia ricocheted off the unfortunate gentleman to trip and fall, Verity found her arms pinned to her sides for one outraged second before she was released and the gentleman was helping Julia up.

'I do beg your pardon,' said Julia, directing the full force of an anxious, repentant smile at him. 'That was entirely our own fault. Pray do not let us detain you. I hope you are not hurt?'

There was good reason why Julia had always been the one to open the apologies when they got into a youthful scrape. The gentleman, though he clearly considered himself the most important person in the street, gave her a single appraising look, murmured '*not at all*' and directed a footman to gather up their fallen possessions before stepping into his curricle and nodding for his groom to pull away.

'That was Sir Philip Munro,' said Julia. 'Did you see the cut of his coat? And the fit and the material? Quite superb. He must fence, do you not think?'

'Undoubtedly,' murmured Verity, remembering the iron grip on her arms. It was easy to see why he excelled as a thief-taker. Had he thought *they* were thieves, perhaps? One to distract, the other to lift the contents of his pockets? She recalled Charles's expression had flattened when he saw Sir Philip at the exhibition. Silently she agreed with him. She did not like the gentleman either.

16

Charles came to Grosvenor Street fully prepared to be extremely cross if the message Verity had for him could have been confided to paper.

'At last,' she said, smiling up at him. 'I began to think I would never see you again.'

She was shameless. Two days apart and he was as undone as ever. He might as well have spared himself the pain of imagining where she was and who she was with.

'I believe I mentioned that I work for a living?' he said, striving for an elder-brotherly tone.

She patted the seat next to her. 'So you did, on which head you must make a note that I have accompanied my mother on an inspection of what she hopes will be her new abode and enquired most diligently into the state of the attics and drains. Your sister and I have made a thorough investigation of a charitable endeavour that aims to relieve ladies in distress by lifting them out of poverty.'

'House hunting and shopping. Tell me this mysterious message that has come your way.'

'It was given to me by Mr Grimes the hackney driver, and it comes from Molly Turner. It is to advise you to talk to Susan Norris in the Bridewell with all dispatch. If you are asked, the information did not come from Molly.'

'And why would your canny friend think this might be to my advantage?'

'I do not know. May I come with you, Charles? Mr Grimes said ladies do sometimes go there for charitable purposes. It will convince my Harrington relations of my sobriety.'

'Rather more so than the Soho Bazaar,' said Charles. 'I cannot like it, Verity. Bridewell is a house of correction. Many of the inmates have been brought there by desperate straits.'

'Were you listening to nothing I said two nights ago? If I have not seen these straits for myself, how can I judge how to help?'

He looked at her with reluctant admiration. 'You do not consider me an able reporter?'

Before he could move away, she touched his cheek gently. 'No, for you are foolish and chivalrous and would try to protect my sensibilities.'

He covered her hand and returned it to her lap. 'Very well, but you will behave.'

'I shall be a model of decorum.'

'That I wish I may live to see,' replied Charles. 'I will call for you in the morning.'

'Will you not stay to dine today?'

'I have work to do.' He hesitated. 'And besides, I dare not.'

'But Mama will be returning soon, and Julia will recover from her sulks and be down shortly. She is cross with me for not lending her the money to buy a reticule.'

'That I do not believe.'

'It would have been wasteful, Charles. She has two blue reticules already.'

'Oh, I believe that. What I cannot credit is that she is cross with you. Julia is never cross. Does she imagine she is being discreet?'

'Your sister sees most things, Charles, even if she is not always sound in her conclusions.'

'I am your attorney, Verity. Do stop making things difficult.'

'Papa used to say his attorney was worth more than he was.'

'He has been practising many years. Mr Tweedie is far from impecunious. I, however, do not command anything like his salary. I cannot support anyone bar myself.'

'Plus your valet and his mother and his simpleton sister. I am not asking you to support me.'

'I will not be accused of marrying for money.'

For answer, Verity lifted her face and kissed him feather-light on the lips. Her action set off a storm of emotions in his chest. His arms came around her of their own volition before he forced them back to his sides.

'I asked you to behave,' he managed in a hoarse voice.

'That was in thanks for tomorrow. Please do not pretend, Charles. Do you not wish to kiss me?'

'I wish it very much, which is why I am leaving now while I can yet walk.' But still he didn't move, knowing exactly how she would feel in his arms, how she would taste, how she would give herself willingly, confident in his ability to teach her.

She kissed him again, less lightly this time, and rose. 'You are being perfectly ridiculous,' she said, a shake in her voice, and left the room.

★　★　★

'You can stop being discreet,' said Verity, sinking dispiritedly on to the window seat in Julia's room. 'You might

288

just as well have been in the salon with us.' Although if she had, Verity might not have found the courage to kiss Charles like that. A furious blush came to her cheeks to think of herself being that forward. Oh, but it had been lovely. And that one moment, when he nearly responded . . . Verity had almost forgotten to breathe.

Julia sighed in sympathy. 'It will be the money. Charles is the most principled of my brothers. He is also the one most likely to ride to the rescue if one is in trouble. Could you pretend to be abducted?'

Verity gave her a dry look. 'Having first had the presence of mind to write him a note telling him where I have been confined? I shall see if I can contrive to throw myself into his lap in the carriage tomorrow.' *And he will put me aside like an irritating harlot and tell me to behave myself.*

A knock on the door heralded a footman with a parcel. 'This was delivered for you, Miss Julia.'

Julia brightened up at once. 'I adore surprises. I hope it is not from Lieutenant Neville or I will be obliged to return it.'

It was not from the lieutenant. Julia carefully undid the sheets of tissue paper to reveal . . .

'It is the reticule,' she gasped. 'Did you go back for it, Verity?'

'When would I have had the time? Besides, you do not need it. Is there a note?'

Julia poked amongst the wrappings and unfolded a crisp sheet of paper. 'Here,' she said, passing it across.

'*To Miss Congreve*,' Verity read aloud. '*Sir Philip Munro begs Miss Congreve to accept this trifle as the inadvertent cause of her tumble on his steps and trusting she is none the worse for it.* Julia, it is from Sir Philip Munro!'

The two friends stared at each other in consternation. 'I cannot return it,' said Julia. 'That would be the height of bad manners. But I do not see how I can accept it either.'

'Perhaps he feels bad about taking us for pickpockets. But Julia, if he heard what we were arguing about then he must have been much more aware of us than he showed.' Verity looked at the reticule uneasily. 'I do not think I like such control.'

'Nor I, though it is flattering that he has gone to the trouble of searching out the reticule and discovering my direction. I am glad it was not as expensive as the work deserves. I do not need to feel guilty about his laying out too great a sum of money.' Julia stroked the blue embroidered satin. 'The best solution is a note, I think, thanking him for his gift and saying it was not in the least necessary. Oh, how annoying gentlemen are. Not only has he robbed us of the excuse to go back there, I dare not even use the reticule, in case he sees me at the next party and reads more into my carrying it than that it goes with my costume.'

'You will have to forswear blue for a

twelvemonth. Shall we send the letter now? We can couch it in a formal style to match his. I have paper and a good pen in my writing case.'

'You are the best of friends.'

Verity made a rueful face. 'If I had been a better one, I would have lent you the money, and then we would not have had to deal with this at all.'

★ ★ ★

She told Charles about the incident the next morning in an effort to banish embarrassment and keep the atmosphere friendly.

'Odd,' said Charles, frowning. 'I hope he is not getting a *tendre* for Julia. I do not trust a man who turns thieves in for sport. It bespeaks a lack of emotion.'

'She does not return the regard. I thought you should know in case he referred to either the gift or Julia's tripping on his step in conversation. It did not strike me that he looked at you in the gallery with any degree of goodwill.'

'Nor I him. He is a difficult gentleman to like. Too remote, though I may be wronging him. How do you get on with the furnishings for Furze House? The lease is now signed. There seems no reason why you and Kitty should not remove there as soon as we can get her safely away.'

He was clearly desperate to evict her from his orbit. Verity answered in the same composed tone, but having regarded Charles as a friend her whole life, her heart was breaking to think he might never be anything more. Men, as Julia said, were unfathomable.

At the Bridewell, he became more like himself. 'Stay close, Verity, and strive for an open mind. Many of the wretches here have very little choice in life. Much can be forgiven the poor.'

They went through an archway and across a walled yard. It was large and open to the sky, but the high walls gave Verity an oppressed feeling similar to when she was lost in the fog. A small window set in a door gave her a glimpse of a large bare room with straw piled in wooden frames for beds, and then they were shown into a small room, where two young women and a child were brought in. One woman settled herself on a chair with the babe on her knee and looked Charles boldly in the eye. The other huddled in a corner, head bent, wrapping her arms around her body as if she would never be warm.

'Susan Norris,' said the warder, 'and the woman brought in with her. She'll not leave her, though you'll not get any sense from her.'

'Her name is Hannah,' said Susan Norris pointedly. 'She'll do no harm. And what can I do for you, my fine fellow? Can you get me out of here?'

The warder made to strike her, but Charles spread his hand.

'My name is Congreve, Miss Norris,' he said. 'I know nothing except I am to talk to you. Perhaps you could start by relating how you came to be in this place.'

'One moment.' Verity could not bear the other woman's silent shivering any longer. She crossed to Hannah's chair and wrapped her own shawl around her. 'Please, take this if it will help.'

Hannah looked up, fearful and startled. Verity was shocked at how young she was, younger even than herself. 'Thank you, miss,' she whispered.

Susan Norris looked across with good-humoured impatience. 'Now I'll have to stop them robbing her of it, no doubt, but you meant well, miss. Plenty don't.'

'Your story, Miss Norris?' asked Charles.

'Vagrants, they are.' The warder spat on the floor.

'Vagrants nothing. Temporarily without a situation on account of a fire at old Mother McCarthy's last week and us losing all our worldly goods.'

'You were at Mother McCarthy's?

The . . . ' Charles darted a wary look at Verity. 'The, er, accommodation house in Hart Street?'

Susan gave a broad grin. 'Aye, very accommodating we are. Not that I wouldn't rather be dressing hair given half a chance, but there you are. You have to take what's slopped out to you in this life, don't you?'

Verity was forcibly reminded of Molly Turner and thus had a suspicion of what might go on behind the doors of an accommodation house, but nothing could have prepared her for the tale Susan told.

'It's like this. Two years ago, I was a lady's maid down in Kent and if I'd known then what I know now, I'd have stayed that way, no matter how much I was sweet-talked by him as was courting my young lady. Mr Weston, his name was, a bit older than you, sir, lovely looking. Not a female in the place whose heart didn't race that bit faster when he smiled. He was after my mistress and her money, but it was me he really wanted. Talked about when they was married and in a nice house, him and me could have an arrangement on the side. It wasn't wicked, my mistress would never know, and that way I'd have a place for life. He could charm the cream right out of the milk, could Mr Weston.'

Huddled in Verity's shawl, Hannah gave a dismal sob.

'Well, the master saw which way the land lay and forbid Mr Weston the house. Mr Weston came to me laughing, and says he can bear losing my lady, but his heart was awful sore at leaving me behind. Would I come with him? We could go to London. He'd show me St Paul's. He'd take me to Vauxhall and Ranelagh and we'd dance the night away under the stars. We might even get married, what did I say to that? Well, nobody ever packed a bag faster. I ran away with him that very night. We rented a room at Mother McCarthy's and were as happy as two partridges in a pie — and then a week later, off he goes to find work and I never saw him again.'

Verity, who had sat up straight at the mention of Vauxhall and Ranelagh, felt her mouth make an 'ooh' of surprise.

Susan shrugged. 'After another week, Mother McCarthy comes up to my room. Said she needed rent right now or I was out on the street. Alternatively, if I wouldn't mind obliging a gentleman friend of hers, the same way I'd obliged Mr Weston, she'd take the rent money off him and give me what was left over. I figured I was pretty much ruined by then, so why not. By the time I found out just how many gentleman friends she had, and talked to some of the other girls who rented rooms off her and realised what sort of a house it was, I was swelling with the babe here and it was too late to get a respectable position.'

'That's dreadful,' said Verity, horrified.

'I had harsh words in my head for Mr Weston, that's for sure. Come forward to three or four months ago. I'd waved off my latest gent and was going to tell Mother McCarthy to give me an hour to feed and change the babe, when the street door opens and who do I see at the bottom of the stairs but Mr Weston, with Hannah here tucked into his arm. I drew back pretty fast, you can be sure of that. 'Have you got a room free, Mother?' he asks, and she starts to show them up to the one opposite mine. Well, I shuts my door, and gets on with sorting out my little one. Bless me, but it was only two hours later when I heard the door opposite open and close quietly and then there were footsteps on the stairs. I crept to the stairwell and listened. He and Mother McCarthy were talking in the hall, but she's so stingy with the candles, neither of 'em could have seen me up above.'

'And what did they say?' asked Charles.

Hannah wept a fresh volley of sobs into the shawl.

'Give over,' said Susan. 'He's lost to

both of us now. Don't you want him to get what's coming to him?' She looked back at Charles. 'He tells her Hannah's asleep, a soft enough handful but nothing much to recommend her, and he'd take his usual ten guineas, please, and he'd clear off out of the way.'

'The monster!' gasped Verity.

'Old McCarthy started Hannah on the gentlemen the very next night. She didn't take to it like me, so Mother figured if she was going to weep the whole time, she might as well give her to the vicious ones who like a bit of pain. Not right, it wasn't. Fair turned my stomach to hear it. She could've put Hannah to the scullery or kitchens where she'd have been happy enough skiving, but no. Those gents pay more, see?'

'Despicable,' said Charles, looking grim. 'How did you get away?'

Susan shrugged. 'There was a fire. Smoke everywhere and all the girls shrieking. I gathered up the babe, grabbed Hannah and we ran out the back way. Got picked up and took to Bow Street where I told 'em everything I've told you. That's when they said they'd never heard of no Mr Weston, nor yet Mr North, which was the name he gave when he was courting Hannah's young lady. They was right interested in what I had to say about Mother McCarthy, mind.'

'Mr North?' said Verity, looking with wild surmise at Charles.

He looked back at her, sharing the triumph. 'Got him,' he said softly.

17

After leaving the women with assurances that something would be done about Mr Weston and that the pair would be found a suitable situation together, Charles and Verity emerged into a city where the very air seemed a deal more wholesome than that inside.

Verity took a deep breath, savouring the freshness. 'Are all prisons like that?'

'Most are far worse. At least in the Bridewell women can keep their babies and the poor have access to medicines. It was good of you to give Susan money for better food.'

'How could I not? But Charles, I thought Mr Weston would be Lieutenant Neville when Susan mentioned him promising to take her to Vauxhall and Ranelagh. I was so surprised it was Captain Eastwick. He seems to like compass names, doesn't he?'

'Lieutenant Neville?' said Charles. 'Why?'

'He offered to take me there — almost with that same phrase. It was one of the things that annoyed me so much at the Stanhopes' party.'

'Why did you not tell me?'

'When did I have a chance? You were too busy stealing my heart when we danced and then being noble and staying away from me for days and days.' She could not help colouring as she said this, but he was being so very stubborn that she had to get a response out of him somehow.

'Verity, you are impossible.'

'It is true, nevertheless. Did you not like dancing with me?'

'Very much. I like dancing with you, I like walking with you, I like the feeling of your weight on my arm, but it would be in every way improper for me to take matters further.'

'How so? Uncle James would consider marriage to a sensible, hard-working gentleman eminently rational behaviour. It would solve all our problems in one stroke.'

'Proposing to an impecunious attorney is *not* rational, however. And if you could refrain from using the word stroke, I would be grateful. May we consider the problem of Captain Eastwick instead?'

'Charles, are you blushing?' asked Verity, charmed.

'Behave,' he said, but his lips twitched and he had to look away from her.

Verity desisted, well pleased with the result of her provocation. 'What can we do about Captain Eastwick? Can we lay information? Charles, has he been boasting to his gambling circle, do you think? Might Lieutenant Neville have overheard him in one of the clubs where he plays cards? The coincidence of that wording is quite extraordinary.'

'It's possible. He visits a great many gambling dens. The drawback to laying information *now* about his treatment of those young women is that he will deny it and be bound over to appear another day. Then he will disappear and your sister will be looking over her shoulder for the rest of her life.'

Verity nodded soberly. 'Is there nothing can we do? We cannot simply leave it, Charles.'

'I have no intention of leaving it. We need to confront him, I think, with plenty of witnesses. While he is distracted, we could get your sister and her little girl away from London. I have a friend who can help us, a gentleman who on the surface has no connection with either me or you. When do you see Kitty again?'

'They are to visit Mama today.'

'Then I shall deliver you home and perhaps stay for a dutiful nuncheon with my parents.'

'They will be astonished.'

'Unlike my clerk, who has quite given up seeing me in chambers at all. He was complaining yesterday that between me and Mr Tweedie, we barely make one full person's work.'

'I own I was surprised when Mr Tweedie stayed so long at Kensington. He was determined Mama should not make an unwise decision.'

'More likely avoiding his domestic upsets. His landlady has imported her niece, who has lost her own position. She is very modern and comes complete with a husband and young family. It is all being quite a trial and not what he is used to in the least.'

'Poor Mr Tweedie. No wonder he was so eager to dine with us on the day of the fog. Goodness, Charles, we have walked nearly all the way home. We were talking so hard I had not noticed. You are a very comfortable person to walk with, not like Julia who is always looking around and commenting on the people and who is coming out of which house.'

'Unless she is arguing with you and banging into them.'

Verity shuddered. 'Pray do not remind me. I do not like him, but I was mortified Sir Philip thought us thieves.

I can still feel his grip on my arms. He was so fast!'

★　★　★

Charles listened to his mother's discourse with every appearance of interest as he watched Verity, Julia and Kitty converse in quick low voices on the other side of the room. He saw the moment Verity told her sister about Captain Eastwick's treatment of Susan Norris and Hannah. Kitty's face turned ashen and her hand flew to her mouth. It was some minutes before she regained enough command over herself to speak.

He murmured an excuse to his mother and crossed to where the ladies were sitting.

Verity made a space for him on the sofa without turning to see him approach. 'She will come to us,' she said.

Charles nodded. 'You have my sympathy, Mrs Eastwick. It is no light thing to discover your husband to be an unprincipled blackguard.'

'I always knew him to be unprincipled,' she replied in a choked voice. 'I knew he collected money from these houses, though I thought he passed that on, and I knew what the houses were. How could I not, when he has also used me on occasion? I swear I thought the women willing, as others of my friends are. I had not realised him to be so evil towards innocents.' Her throat worked again. 'And all for a transient monetary gain, gone on the turn of a card. Ann and I will be ready whenever you send word.'

'You cannot bring much with you,' he warned. 'It is important not to arouse his suspicions if he sees things missing from their accustomed place.'

She made a dismissive gesture. 'There is little I need to pack. I have not so many good clothes that I will notice their loss. The only important item apart from Ann's old rag doll is the cookery book Mama gave me when I was to marry Mr Prout. It saved my life. I brought it away with me as a reminder of her when we eloped, but then discovered it to be the most necessary thing I possessed when I found myself with no cook, no maid and no money. It was the only time I flew at Simon, when I found he had taken it. I screamed at him that if he did not pawn something else and get my *Domestic Cookery* back — my book, no other — then he would starve just as surely as me and have nowhere to bring his card-playing friends. I said the only way that book would leave me again was if I went first in a coffin.' She gave the ghost of a shrug, her eyes bleak. 'I paid the price later, but I got it back.'

Charles did not question her further. 'To bring this off with any degree of success neither Verity nor I should be seen to be involved, so it will be a friend of mine who comes for you, and it will be at a time when your husband is not at home. What period of the day is best?'

'He is in and out during the morning, but generally for longer in the afternoon. I used to believe that was when he settled down to fleece young men of their pocketbooks. Now I do not know what to think.'

Verity pressed her hand sympathetically.

'I will tell Nick to keep a watch on your address,' said Charles. 'He will give you a codeword, something to the effect that he is interested in a rare cookery book. Will that suffice?'

Kitty Eastwick nodded. 'Will it be soon? It is not that I cannot live a lie for much longer, knowing what I do now — it is that I think Simon is more than usually in need of finance, so his actions may be unpredictable. He asked me yesterday how much Mama would pay to take Ann and bring her up. I do not dare contemplate what else he might do. If I could leave her here, I would, but he will be waiting for us on Piccadilly and would doubtless march me straight back to demand payment should I meet him without her.'

'He would sell his own child? Good God, he is a monster.'

Kitty's voice became little more than a whisper. 'I believe so indeed. He must have loved me once, to have married me with no dowry, but that has long passed.'

'It will be within the week,' promised Charles. He thought for a moment. 'I begin to have an idea. I will walk with you when you leave, then go on to my chambers. It will do no harm to show you are not without friends.'

'We will come too as we did before, but we cannot accompany you beyond Bond Street,' said Verity. 'He and Julia must not meet or he will realise his history is known.'

'I could wish you *both* as far away as possible,' said Charles with feeling.

★ ★ ★

'We will see you soon, I hope,' said Verity at the end of the road. She kissed

311

Ann and hugged her sister.

Kitty returned the embrace. 'He is a good man, your Mr Congreve,' she murmured in Verity's ear. 'Do not let him get away.'

'I won't. He is stubborn and full of pride, but I have every hope of wearing him down.'

They waved them off. Verity took a moment to admire the straightness of Charles's back as he walked beside Kitty and Ann.

Julia linked arms with her. 'Sometimes Charles can be very blind. I shall be pleased to call you a sister in name, as well as in spirit.'

'He has not even admitted he loves me,' said Verity. 'I believe he wishes Furze House to be settled as much to pack me off there as to provide Kitty with a refuge. Oh Julia, those poor women. How can anyone be treated so cruelly? I keep seeing Hannah, huddled and terrified, in my head.'

Julia looked sombre. 'She brought the hot water and the morning tea at the

Cattsons' house. She was not bright, but willing and enjoyed her work. Would she go to Furze House with you? Would she be content with Kitty living there? If not, I could ask Mama to give her a place with us.'

'I don't know. She shook when Charles spoke, as gentle as he is. She would be happier in a household of women, and happier too, back in the country.' Verity bit her lip. 'So many women, Julia, all deceived. How many more might there be? I begin to be sick of London. So much glitter on the surface and misery underneath. I shall be glad to go back to Newmarket. Perhaps when I am no longer within Charles's vision and causing him trouble every day, he will realise he misses me.'

'It is possible,' said Julia. 'Men are unfathomable. It is a wonder they manage to run the world at all. I will miss you though. How am I to carry through all my intrigues without you to scold me into better behaviour?'

'You must practise restraint, Julia, or I shall return to find the hallway knee-deep in reticules and the street outside littered with the decaying remains of baronets and officers of His Majesty's army.'

Julia considered this. 'It's not an *unattractive* prospect . . . '

★ ★ ★

Charles made polite conversation after Julia and Verity left them. Scanning ahead, he appreciated the reason for Captain Eastwick choosing Piccadilly as a meeting place. All along the road were gentlemen lounging in doorways or standing idly passing the time in knots of two or three.

'There is Papa,' said Kitty to Ann. And to Charles, 'He is in front of Savory and Moore, which strikes me as appropriate. There have been times when I have been tempted to go in and buy their entire stock of laudanum.' She took a shallow breath. 'But no more.'

'He is talking to Freddy,' observed the child. 'Freddy is a fast runner, isn't he? I saw him when we came out of Grandmama's house.'

'That is not her own house, Ann. She is staying there with a friend. Now remember, you are not to mention anything of our conversation today, except that you helped sort out her pretty silks and ate a great many bonbons.'

'No, Mama.'

Charles felt a surge of fury at the pinched, adult look on Kitty's daughter's face. Children of six should be happy and laughing, not old before their time. 'Will you introduce me?' he said abruptly.

'Certainly,' replied Kitty. As they drew level with the chemist's shop, she stood a little taller and said in a cool, social voice. 'There you are, Simon. I wondered if we might see you on our way back. Mr Congreve, might I introduce my husband, Captain Eastwick? Simon, Mr Congreve is the attorney I told you of who is overseeing my sister's legacy. He is returning to the Temple and very kindly offered to escort us along part of our way.'

'It was no trouble,' said Charles, managing to sound polite, but harried. He nodded to Eastwick. 'Pleased to make your acquaintance. You'll forgive me hurrying off. I have a great many things to attend to, which Miss Bowman's affairs are unfortunately taking precedence over.'

He resolutely did not look back to see how Eastwick comported himself with his wife, but made his way to his chambers with all despatch. He needed to send a note to Nicholas Dacre, and had also to think up a plan to accidentally meet and distract Eastwick for long enough that Nick might get Kitty safely away. If the man habitually lounged along Piccadilly, this might be easier than he'd expected. On the edge of his consciousness was that as she'd turned to go, Julia had reminded him not to be late to dine. He hadn't the remotest notion why. It was Verity's fault, she was invading his every thought and turning him into a tattered semblance of his previously organised self. The sooner she was safely in Newmarket the better. Then he might regain acceptance of his chosen lot. He determined there and then that if he *was* engaged to escort them somewhere tonight, he would confine his dealings with her to polite conversation only.

On turning into the building where his chambers were situated, he was so lost in deliberations as to how to achieve this impossible resolve that he ran into a large gentleman striding through the archway just ahead of him.

'Adam!' he cried, belatedly recognising his friend. 'By all that's wonderful. You are the very man I need.'

Adam Prettyman grinned. 'That's flattering. You won't say it when you know my purpose. Jenny has entrusted me with a great long list of household linen that I am to purchase while I am signing these new leases we discussed.'

Charles waved this away as an irrelevancy. 'Verity and Julia have been buying little else for days. We can recruit them to the cause. You, however . . . How do you fancy reviving your thespian past and playing a naive country fellow with money in his pocket? There is a certain card-sharp of my acquaintance who would be delighted to relieve you of it.'

'Nothing I should like more. I take it this is not the shadowy gentleman you were telling me of?'

'Sadly no, he remains as concealed within his web as ever. My unsavoury quarry is Verity's half-sister's husband. He is a monster who deserves to rot in Newgate for as long as I can keep him there. Come up and I will explain. I must also pen a letter to a friend and check on a report of a gambling den I paid insufficient attention to when I was told of it a few days ago. It might be the very place for my purpose, provided we sit near a door.'

Adam smiled. 'You never cease to

surprise me, Charles. Tell me, do you get any of your regular work done at all?'

'Not according to my clerk. He has reason. I am particularly distracted at the moment.'

'I am all ears.'

18

'So that is my plan,' said Charles. He had brought Adam to dine at Grosvenor Street where Verity had been delighted to see him. She was looking more bewitching than ever this evening, as if she was purposely ignoring what he had told her about an attorney not being able to give his wife the life he would like her to have. 'Tonight we will take part in whichever entertainment Julia has decided is good for us and Adam will give his impression of a country bumpkin out on the town. Tomorrow, with your help, we will first see to Jenny's commissions, and then he and I will look for divertissement in Captain Eastwick's favourite gambling hell. From what your sister said, I doubt he will be averse to taking money off us.'

Julia made a dissatisfied grimace.

'You will have to go to the linen warehouse without me. Mama and I are promised to our eldest brother's wife for the day. As it is in a noble cause, I shall be very kind and mention how hard you are working, Charles.'

'Thank you,' said Charles gravely. Then he frowned. 'Will Mrs Bowman be at home, Verity? We are arranging for my friend Nicholas Dacre — whom you do not know, Julia, and I will be obliged if you instantly forget his name — to collect Kitty as soon as her husband leaves the house and to bring her and the child here.'

Verity met his eyes, a wrinkle of worry in them. 'Yes, Mama will be in, for she is expecting Mr Tweedie to call about the Kensington villa. I will ask them to put off going again to look at it until I return. I am glad you are to rescue Kitty so soon, but is Grosvenor Street not the first place Captain Eastwick will search for her?'

Charles exchanged a look with Adam. 'I am hoping he will have rather more on his mind by the time he discovers she is gone. Even if I cannot detect that he is cheating at cards, I intend taking him in charge for deception over those two women. Both offences count as fraud. Adam and I will disable him and take him to Bow Street. Once he is there, I can arrange for both the women he wronged to give evidence against him.'

Julia had been listening closely. 'If you need a witness of good character, I will say I knew him in Shropshire as Mr North. The Cattsons themselves are in town. The whole family will tell you he was in their house under a false name.'

'I doubt my mother will look kindly on your visiting Bow Street,' said Charles, 'but a written deposition will lend weight.'

Verity jumped up and crossed to the table. 'Excellent idea. For Kitty's sake, I would have him incarcerated as swiftly as possible. I will write the letter now, Julia, and you can sign it. My handwriting is by far more readable and

this way, Charles will have it with him.'
She paused in the act of reaching for a
pen. 'It puzzles me how Captain
Eastwick knew about Miss Cattson and
her fortune. Shropshire is very far away.
What gave him the notion to inveigle
himself into the household?'

'There may have been an announce-
ment in the newspaper of her grandmother's
death. Or possibly the brother mentioned
it in conversation.'

'But he had already introduced
himself to the brother under a false
name. Also, how did he know about the
household in Kent where Susan Norris
was in service? She said he was courting
her mistress. Kitty told me he frequently goes away for weeks at a time,
returning in funds. If he follows the
same pattern every time, where does he
get the information that there is an
heiress whose family will pay him off?
The newspapers cannot always give the
details, surely?'

Charles met her eyes, struck again by
her intelligence and wrenched beyond

belief at the thought that they would really deal very well together if only he had greater financial security. 'It is a valid point. I have been so focused on the outcome of his machinations that I hadn't considered his sources. Could it simply be society gossip?'

Verity shook her head. 'He does not move in society. He does not even come into this part of town.'

'Then it must be the gentlemen he plays cards with. Did you not say Lieutenant Neville's conversation resembles his own? Those men do move in society and depend on it, he will have their names and situations out of them in a matter of minutes under the guise of being a capital, sympathetic fellow. I have seen such blackguards many times. It is one of the ways to tell a sharp before ever he deals a hand.'

'I am more than ever glad I only play round games,' said Julia. She turned to Adam. 'I hope you will not find it too awkward tonight, Adam. My brother has evidently forgotten that we are all bound for the Sans Pareil. The season has just opened. Miss Scott has written a new melodrama, and there is said to be a very fine ballet, as well as the farce.'

Adam smiled. 'That sounds a good programme. Time was I'd have been cribbing the new play for all I was worth so I could reproduce it with the Players. It will be a novelty to simply watch and enjoy.'

Charles retreated into his own thoughts. It was fortunate Julia had changed the subject. The stimulating exchanging of ideas with Verity was doing nothing for his mental equilibrium.

★ ★ ★

The Lord of the Castle was everything a melodrama should be. Verity sat back in satisfaction at the end. She looked around the audience and waved to Lilith Fitzgilbert in a box further along with a party including her brother and stepmother. Access to theatres was something Verity would miss when she returned to Newmarket. Since Adam had disbanded his touring company, they were dependent on the far less frequent visits of the North and South Company of Comedians, unless they went to Bury St Edmunds when the Norwich Company were in the town.

'Oh no,' whispered Julia in consternation. 'Sir Philip Munro is over there and has just looked this way. Quick, Charles, talk to me as if we are discussing the play, or my future prospects, or anything. I need to appear completely absorbed. Did Verity tell you about that wretched reticule?'

Verity hid a smile. Julia's beauty was forever attracting the wrong sort of admirers. It wasn't a problem she herself had ever had. She turned to Adam, asking him for a proper account of Jenny and what it was she required in the way of linen. Nursery furnishings in the main, he said, and made her laugh with a tale of how Jenny had not been feeling well last week and the children had been so determined to be quiet and not disturb her that she hadn't got a moment's rest all afternoon because she was fretting about what mischief they were up to.

After the interval came the ballet with the Sans Pareil's principal dancers, Monsieur and Madam Leclercq. *The Woodman Prince* was very pretty, but it didn't hold Verity's attention as much as the play. She might have enjoyed it more had she been seated next to Charles but he seemed determined to avoid paying her any particular attention this evening. That might suit *him* very well, but it did not forward her designs. Accordingly, when the Fitzgilberts visited their box during the second interval she effected a change of seat with Julia and thus was close to Charles when the farce began.

'*The Sportsman and Shepherd*,' she said, reading the handbill. 'It's useful when a title describes the plot, don't you think? It makes it easier to follow the action if the players are in the habit of mumbling.'

There was a reluctant smile in Charles's eyes. 'Were you bored with Adam's company?' he enquired.

'You know Julia likes to discuss the topical nuances of any play she sees. She thought Adam, from his experience, would be a more informed conversationalist.'

'I could almost believe you if I did not know it would be Julia doing most of the talking. Why are you making this so difficult? Do you really wish to be the butt of society jokes about the gamekeeper marrying the bird in the hand? I am attempting to keep our relationship businesslike for both our sakes.'

'I do not want a businesslike relationship and nor do you at heart. What does it matter whose money a young couple settle down on? Who will care?'

'Me. I care. I would as lief not feel shabby at the start of married life.'

328

'As well not every eligible gentleman feels the same or half the heiresses in the country would be doomed to die old maids, without even the solace of children to comfort them. Do reflect, Charles. We have not even kissed properly. We may not suit, and then we would have had all this honourable suffering for nothing.'

'Oh no, Verity. You are not tricking me like that. If once I kiss you properly, we are both lost.'

She peeped up at him. 'Improperly, then?'

'No! And that is a fact, not a challenge.' He sat back with his arms folded and gazed steadfastly at the stage.

If once I kiss you, we are both lost. Verity's heart danced and leaped inside her chest. She already knew Charles was the only gentleman she would ever accept. That single phrase told her she had been right and he *did* love her in return.

If once I kiss you, we are both lost.

She straightened her shoulders. If that was what it would take, she had best scheme how to achieve it.

★ ★ ★

By next morning, Verity was no nearer a means of bringing Charles to a declaration. There was a great press of people in Grafton House, but with the benefit of many days experience, she had the satisfaction of seeing respect in the men's eyes when she completed Jenny's purchases with dispatch. Adam only wished for a personal present for his wife now, so while he paid for the fabric and arranged its conveyance to Grosvenor Street, she and Charles stepped into the street to hail them all a hackney to Rundell & Bridge. Verity wondered if a lingering look at the plain wedding bands might not go amiss while they were there.

As they left Grafton House, a shout of 'thief' went up inside. A ruckus instantly ensued.

'Oh, not again,' cried Verity, turning to look, only to find herself separated from Charles in the confusion. His place at her side was taken by her brother-in-law. 'Captain Eastwick!' she said in strong surprise, not at all liking the grip he had on her arm.

'Just the lady I was wishful of meeting,' he replied.

He really did have a powerful presence, even out here in the street. She wondered Kitty could stand it. 'What is the matter?' she asked in alarm. 'Is something wrong with my sister?'

'It's more myself I'm concerned with. See to the gentleman, Smith. He is bound to be tiresome and I'd rather not have any delays.'

'Charles?' Verity twisted in alarm to look at him and felt a sudden slice of pain at her waist. 'Ow. What are you . . . ?'

'I wouldn't struggle, my dear. I might hurt you. Things are a little desperate for niceties, I am afraid. Just keep walking.'

331

Her first thought was to pull out of his grip, gather up her skirts and run for safety. Her second thought was that she couldn't because if Captain Eastwick was absent from home, Kitty and Ann might be arriving in Grosvenor Street any moment. Further thoughts were petrified into non-existence by the flash of steel in Captain Eastwick's hand and the realisation of what the increasing pain at her waist had been caused by.

'Careful, Verity, he has a knife,' called Charles urgently. There was a workmanlike set of thuds and then he was on her other side massaging his knuckles. 'Shocking manners your colleague has got, Eastwick. We hadn't even been introduced. Train him yourself, did you?'

'Damn you, Congreve. As you see, I have a blade pressed against Miss Bowman's ribs. If you don't want her blood on your hands, you'll stay out of this.'

'There would be more chance of a river flowing uphill,' said Charles.

'Where are you taking me?' said Verity. She didn't try to keep the fear out of her voice as she was hustled along. If Captain Eastwick thought her cowed, he might relax his hold. Had Adam seen them? He had won prize purses for rough fighting in his younger days. Pray God he was following.

'We are going, my dear sister, to a private establishment I frequent. Your friend Mr Congreve is more than welcome to accompany us. He may lose some money while we are occupied. The whist is of a particularly high standard.'

Occupied? Susan Norris and Hannah came vividly to mind. Perspiration sheeted off her. She faltered, only for another prick from the knife to spur her on. This couldn't be happening. She could not be abducted in broad daylight. Why was Charles not tackling him? It was to his credit that he daren't risk her being injured, but surely it would be far harder to escape once they were at their destination?

'How did you know where I was?' she asked.

Captain Eastwick smiled with satisfaction. 'Errand boys. No one ever notices them. My lad hears you say there's no need for a hackney just to go to Grafton House. He tells me. I come here. Information is currency and there is always someone poorer than oneself. The boy gets a farthing. I stand to get a great deal more.'

Verity's voice rose. 'More? What do you mean? What do you want of me?'

'Not your body, or only in a manner of speaking. I need your money. I owe a considerable sum to a gentleman who is being rather pressing over the repayment. Unfortunately, he has made his displeasure known by disrupting my usual supply of funds. Now, while I am owed a significant amount myself, the fellow who owes me has even less cash than I. He does, however, have his liberty, hence this scheme.'

'You are mistaken, Captain Eastwick. I have no money.' They were hurrying so fast she had lost all sense of direction. Every turn was accompanied by a wrench on her arm or another sharp pain at her waist. She had the ludicrous and fantastically ill-timed thought that if she'd worn long stays this morning rather than a more flattering short laced bodice in order to captivate Charles, she wouldn't be in nearly such a bad way now.

'You have a legacy.' They slowed at last, she was pushed through a narrow alley and into a small, grimy courtyard.

Captain Eastwick opened a door. There was a lantern hook above it, and inside was a cream-painted hallway. The embellishments had originally been picked out in gold. It would still, no doubt, look reasonably opulent by candlelight. In the light of a cold October day, it revealed itself as shabby and in need of a good clean. A menacing individual made to shut the door as soon as they were through, but was thwarted by dint of Charles leaning on it until he too was inside.

'Pray let me go,' said Verity, wishing this was a bad dream she could simply wake up from. 'You are under a misapprehension. My legacy is conditional. I will not be able to benefit from it for six months.'

Captain Eastwick gave a humourless laugh. 'So Kit informed me. A quaint conceit. It will nevertheless be yours once you marry, isn't that how these things are always arranged, Congreve?' He prodded her past an open doorway on the left of the passage where several gentlemen could be seen at play, and indicated a door on the right. 'Behold, madam, your bridegroom.'

The room was stuffy with stale alcohol fumes, and crowded with tables. Soldiers, merchants and gentlemen lounged around them playing at cards, dice or backgammon. At their entrance, one of the officers at the table by the window rose to his feet. He smirked and made an ironic bow. 'We meet again,' he said.

Verity stared in horror at Lieutenant Neville.

'I . . . I cannot . . . '

'I'm afraid you will have to. I cannot stall my creditor any more. Come, it won't be so bad. Neville is nearly as pretty as I was in my heyday, and you've not heard Kit complaining, have you? Stand up straight, girl. The priest is here with a blank licence in his pocket. We'll even clear one of the rooms upstairs for your wedding night.'

Further around the table, Lieutenant Crisp shot to his feet, his fists balled. 'Neville, you blackguard! You said we were here to collect what you owe us. Is this your windfall? The colonel will hear of such an infamous scheme, you may be sure. Miss Bowman, I will escort you home. This is no fit place for you. I am ashamed to be here myself.'

Captain Eastwick signalled to a rough-looking man standing by the wall. The next moment, Peter Crisp was felled with a blow to the temple. Verity pulled away with a cry and pressed herself against Charles's comforting body.

'Unprovoked assault,' said Charles. 'This is quite a litany you're building up.'

Verity turned. 'I cannot wed *anyone*,' she said in a stronger voice. Her side ached abominably, but she daren't look down to see if she was losing blood. 'It is not in my power to do so. Mr Congreve and I are already married.'

'Impossible,' snarled Captain Eastwick. 'You cannot be. I have had the house watched since Kit first told me the address.'

Charles wrapped his left arm around her. 'It was before we left Newmarket,' he replied in a voice so rock-steady any jury in the land would have believed him without question. 'An heiress who is already fond of me is a rare thing, and I didn't quite trust London not to go to my wife's head.'

Verity leaned back against him and looked up. 'Charles,' she said reproachfully.

He smiled down at her. 'Hush. I promised you your Season unencumbered, didn't I?'

There was so much love in his eyes that Verity was dazzled for a moment. Never had she felt so complete. When her brother-in-law snarled in rage, she was furious to have Charles's unvoiced declaration ruined. Any feelings of apprehension for herself came a long way second.

'What of it?' Eastwick grated. 'Neville can marry a widow as well as a virgin. Step aside, sister, lest you are injured.'

For answer, Verity clutched Charles even more firmly.

'Killing me will avail you nothing,' said Charles. 'Mrs Congreve's inheritance has been mine these two weeks and goes to my nephew on my death.'

Captain Eastwick's face turned murderous. Without warning, Verity was yanked back to his side and she yelled in pain. The knife flashed in his hand. 'Then if you wish to keep your wife's pretty skin intact, you will pass the money over now. Two thousand pounds will suffice for the present. More will ensure her life for longer. One of my men will go with you to draw it out.'

'You will have a long wait. I do not have the money yet. You had much better let us go.'

'Borrow against the expectation then. Your credit will be good, though I cannot promise as much for the state of Miss Bowman's — sorry, Mrs Congreve's — person if you tarry too long.'

From the hallway came the sound of male voices as the inhabitants of the other card room pressed into the doorway to see what was happening. Amongst them, Verity saw the enormously reassuring presence of Adam Prettyman, his coat open and his neckerchief loosened as if he'd been there all along.

'How dare you,' she said. 'This is extortion. Any of these men will testify you threatened force to get the money. I refuse to be bargained over like . . . like a stake at cards.'

Please, please let it work. Please let him take the bait. Otherwise Charles will rush him and will surely be killed.

Across the room, Charles's eyes went wide with shock. He understood her.

'Cards,' slurred a voice from the crowded doorway in an accent as unlike Adam's as she had ever heard. 'That's what we're here for, cards.'

'Cards,' repeated Captain Eastwick thoughtfully. He smoothed his hair and his moustache, considered the clasp knife in his hand and looked back at Charles. 'If you are unwilling to borrow the money, what do you say to piquet, Mr Congreve? Three rubbers of six deals each. If you win two out of three, you both walk out of here unmolested. If I win, I have the use of your wife for . . . shall we say a week? I daresay I can make sufficient money from her in that time to cover my debt. Decide quickly, before the stakes rise.' He stroked the tip of his knife down the front of Verity's bodice, watching the material peel easily apart in its wake.

341

Charles's fists bunched. His eyes searched to right and left as if looking for an ally and finding none. 'I'll . . . I'll do it, damn you. But Mrs Congreve sits by my side.'

Captain Eastwick pushed her contemptuously across to him. 'Enjoy her company while you may.'

A table was hauled nearer the centre of the room and Charles and Verity shoved roughly into chairs. Charles pulled off his neck cloth and formed it into a pad that she could hold against her side. As she was searching in her reticule for a ribbon to secure it in place, other seats were pulled up so spectators could watch the game. Verity was aware of expectant heavy breathing behind her. She shuddered and felt for Charles's arm. In contrast to his pretended nervous demeanour, his grip was firm and steady. He withdrew his hand and rested his fingers lightly on the table. Behind him, Verity caught a glimpse of the heavy-breathing gentleman's coat sleeve. She ducked her head, keeping her expression neutral. It was good to know that when Charles won the bet, Adam was at their backs to help them fight their way out of the house.

19

Charles sat at the table, calculating rapidly. This hadn't been how today was supposed to go, but aside from the very real complication of Verity being here and in danger, the situation was close to how he and Adam had planned it. They were in a place where Eastwick felt safe, they were sideways to the door so had a good chance of forcing an exit should it become necessary, and Eastwick was already underestimating Charles's skill.

How long did he have? Eastwick's manner regarding the necessity for finance had been urgent. Had he been referring to the Hart Street brothel fire when he said the gentleman he owed money to had made his displeasure known? If so, Eastwick himself was playing for high stakes. A creditor who thought nothing of firing a building with the residents still inside was not likely to show mercy to a man who defaulted on payment.

So, two tasks. Firstly, Charles had to win the game and have the right to remove himself and Verity, however difficult that last step was going to be in practice. Secondly, he had to arrest Eastwick for deceiving the maids with false promises of marriage and selling them to the brothel. And thirdly, he supposed, he had to get the man to Bow Street.

This was going to be an interesting afternoon.

He did have one slender advantage. Eastwick wasn't the only man to make use of street urchins. As they'd been man-handled through the alley, young Thomas, the coal merchant's son had pelted away in the opposite direction. The longer Charles took over the game, the more time Thomas would have to find Fitz, or explain to Mr Tweedie, or go to Bow Street to say he'd seen them abducted.

As he'd been thinking and helping Verity to fashion a makeshift bandage, he'd studied the cards from the previous game that had been thrown face-down on the table. He was in no doubt that the pack would be marked in some way. This was not a den designed to leave money with its clients. He was equally in no doubt that Eastwick would call for a new pack before they started. However, since making individual plates for the backs of cards was expensive, he'd bet all Eastwick's new packs were printed to the same design.

A gambling den and Eastwick was rattled. Would he follow the card-sharp's customary practice of drawing the victim in gradually and make him think he was winning, before dragging him deeper until the waters closed over his head? Eastwick didn't need to in this case, but if he was on edge and not thinking straight, habit might prevail.

'New cards,' said Eastwick. He broke

the seal with deliberation and met Charles's eyes.

'Ready, Congreve?'

'Ready,' said Charles.

Charles had learned to play piquet at his grandfather's knee, and had taught Julia when his older brothers refused to play with him. It only took two hands for him to identify the markings on the backs of the cards. He could do nothing about the cards in the talon, but he kept his own fan of cards as narrow as possible so his opponent did not get a chance to con them.

He won the first hand easily, declared carte blanche on the second before Eastwick could score a repique, then settled down to decide on the cards he would exchange in the third hand.

In a way it annoyed him that the cards were marked. When piquet was played properly, it was a reasonably simple matter to deduce where each card lay. Charles had realised from the outset that Eastwick was an experienced player. He shouldn't need to cheat. Was he lazy, perhaps? Had he been cheating for so long that his intellect was blunted? In short, without markings to rely on, might his discard process be rusty?

Beside him, Verity pressed a hand to her side. If she had cracked a whip, Charles's resolve couldn't have crystallised any faster. What was he thinking? This wasn't an ordinary game. He didn't have the luxury of treating it as an intellectual exercise. He was playing for her life!

Brain and fingers working smoothly in concert, Charles knew his best chance was to unsettle Eastwick and fool him into miscalculating. He was already hiding the tops of his cards and arranging them haphazardly in his hand rather than organising them by suit. Now he would vary the pace as well. He began to play faster. Eastwick retaliated by playing slower until the onlookers started chaffing him by making bets on when his next card would be laid down. Provoked, he made a mistake and

Charles took the hand.

At the end of the first rubber, Charles was the winner by a narrow margin. He didn't trouble to hide how relieved he was. Eastwick might read strung-nerves into his demeanour and hopefully surprise at his own luck. That was all to the good. The more his opponent misjudged his skill the better. Now, should he go all out to win the second rubber, or could he afford to take it easier?

His heart said to push ahead. He wanted to win the bet and get Verity out of this foul place. His head, however, pointed out the unlikelihood of their being allowed to walk free, bet or no bet. And what of the arrest? Unlike the more high-class clubs, this den was sprinkled with Eastwick's own thugs. Unless Fitz by some miracle managed to arrange the dispatch of a couple of Bow Street Runners here, there was very little chance of them bringing off a second coup.

Deal by deal, the points crept up in

Charles's favour. The quality of his own play was spurring Eastwick to rekindle the skill he'd presumably had in his early days, before he relied on marked cards and games that were biased in the house's favour. An unlucky deal on the penultimate hand gave Eastwick the chance to score heavily. So be it. If this rubber went against him, then the third would give him the extra time he needed to lull Eastwick's suspicions and plan his final actions. It might even bring reinforcements. Across the room, Lieutenant Crisp had recovered. He might be ineffectual in the drawing room, but by the look in his eyes, he was itching to take down a few of what he clearly now saw as the enemy. That could be useful, provided the man was quick enough on the uptake to see where his help would do most good.

The last deal of the rubber. Outwardly languid, Eastwick's eyes were taking note of every card he dealt, spreading the twos and threes in order to see the tiny details on the corner curlicues. Charles watched him stolidly, his attention sharpening as small beads of sweat broke out on his opponent's brow. Eastwick laid down the talon. As his eyes fell on the back of the topmost card, his lips moved soundlessly in a curse.

Charles picked up his cards in silence. Just a glimpse showed him the reason for Eastwick's despair. It was a well-nigh perfect hand. It only needed the addition of the Jack of clubs and the Ace of diamonds to give him a repique and a capot to boot. A flickering glance told him the top card on the talon was indeed the missing club honour. There was no way he could throw this hand. He exchanged his minor cards, watched Eastwick exchange his, and saw ruin sit down next to his enemy.

This was it. Charles didn't have the leisure of another rubber to plan his moves. He was going to have to act the moment he won the bet. At his shoulder, he heard Adam take a long breath.

'Point of seven,' he said.

'Good,' replied Eastwick, his voice remote.

'Septième.'

'Good.'

'Quatorze of aces.'

A ripple went around the room.

Eastwick leaned back. 'Good,' he said.

As Charles took trick after trick he tried to guess which way Eastwick would jump. He laid down the last one, claimed the rubber, the game and the win.

Led by Adam, the spectators stirred, claiming their own side-bets off each other. Adam himself stretched and ambled around the table.

It was time to act. 'I made an interesting acquaintance the other day,' Charles said casually. 'Two interesting acquaintances, to be accurate.'

'The devil you did,' replied Eastwick. His eyes flicked to a couple of people behind Charles.

Charles drew Verity closer to him.

'Yes indeed. Two ladies who had been made homeless when their building in Hart Street was set on fire whilst they and their fellow residents were inside.'

He had Eastwick's attention now, the charm long gone, his face a mask of calculation. 'What of it?'

Charles's words fell like an executioner's blade. 'Both of them had been lured to London with promises of marriage. Both of them had been sold into prostitution. The gentleman in both cases was you. I am arresting you for . . . '

Eastwick gave a feral cry and stood up at the exact moment when Adam pinioned his arms to his sides. 'Smith,' he yelled, struggling to no avail.

Charles laughed at the vindictive punch with which Lieutenant Crisp felled the bully who had laid him out earlier. 'I suggest, gentlemen,' he said, raising his voice to address the company, 'that you all go back to your tables, or find yourselves elsewhere. Captain Eastwick, alias Mr Weston, alias Mr North, has a pressing appointment at Bow Street. Lieutenant Crisp, I wonder if you would be kind enough to relieve the captain of his pistol and a particularly nasty clasp-knife. It would not surprise me if there were other weapons on his person.'

All the time he was talking, he had kept Verity next to him. A desperate litany in his head was praying that Eastwick would stay in a state of shock for long enough to get him to the rotation house several streets away. Two handkerchiefs did to tie the man's wrists together. Strong as he was, Adam couldn't keep him immobile all the way there.

Eastwick twisted and cursed, but not as much as Charles had expected. Perhaps — with the bet lost and no hope of raising what he owed — being publicly committed for trial was the better option, because then he wouldn't have to face his creditor.

They pushed through the doorway, through the alley that was blessedly unguarded and Charles called down further blessings on the coal merchant's son's head. Not only was the boy's father in the street outside with his cart, some three or four of the other men Charles had helped over the years had added themselves to the crowd of onlookers. There were also several hackney cabs, the drivers peering across the heads of the small throng. The news had evidently spread faster than fire in a tinder-dry summer.

Afterwards, he admitted he lost concentration for a few crucial seconds. The strain of keeping up the facade, of playing a game of piquet on which his and Verity's lives depended, had taken effect. As they pushed through the crowd to the cart, Eastwick staggered in front of him and went down.

'It's a trick,' Charles shouted at once. 'Stay back.'

But it wasn't. As people drew away from the fallen man like ripples retreating from a thrown pebble, a pool of red was seen to stain Eastwick's clothing. Verity gasped and ran to him. She bent her head to his, laying her hand on his chest, then looked up at Charles, stricken. 'He ... he is dead.'

★ ★ ★

Verity didn't know what made her do it. Kitty's husband was a loathsome man, selfish and unprincipled, but the sight of him sprawled unmoving in the road had propelled her forward. She laid a tentative hand on his waistcoat and bent her cheek to his mouth to see if she could detect a breath.

Simon Eastwick's laboured whisper shuddered into her soul. 'Kit's book. Get him.'

She jerked away in shock and saw his eyes glaze. She almost felt his life-force depart. 'He ... he is dead,' she said, scrambling to her feet and backing away. The gash in her side made her gasp in pain. She put a hand to it and then instinctively looked down at the blood seeping from Eastwick's back on to the ground.

That could have been me. A great wave of nausea roiled through her. She staggered and fell blindly into Charles's arms. He held her close: safe, warm, solid and comforting.

'Hush,' he said. 'I've got you.' Then he raised his voice. 'God knows he's no loss, but who did it? Did anyone see?'

Never let me go. Take me home and never let me go. The thought was so loud in her head she must surely have said it aloud. Then she heard Captain Eastwick's final words again.

Kit's book. Get him.

'We have to find Kitty,' she breathed into Charles's coat.

He gave no outward sign of having heard, but said, 'Adam, I must take Verity back to Grosvenor Street. Will you take charge here? Tell the authorities I'll answer any questions they have later.'

'I'll do it,' said Lieutenant Crisp. 'My men will help. Get Mrs Congreve away.

This is no place for a lady.' He started to direct the bystanders, filling out his uniform with the natural authority that had been so absent in the drawing room or at the card table.

Mrs Congreve. Verity swallowed. That was another coil to unravel.

They pushed through the crowd to the hackney cabs.

'Oh, Mr Grimes, is that you?' Verity recognised the patient horse nearest her.

'It is, miss. Missus, I should say. Wish you joy, sir. Grosvenor Street, is it?'

'I'll join you once I've given the lad here a hand,' said Adam to Charles.

Within seconds they were on their way. 'What did he say?' asked Charles.

That was the miraculous thing about Charles. She never had to explain. 'Just four words. *Kit's book. Get him.* I'm scared, Charles.' The hackney juddered over a loose cobble and she cried out in pain again.

Charles cursed himself for not cushioning her. 'How bad is it?' He looked down at where her hand was pressed to her side and the bloodstain on her gown.

'I don't know. I haven't dared to look. I pressed your pad against it and hoped it would suffice. It felt like a line of fire at first. That's what comes of being vain and wearing short stays. If I'd worn long ones, nothing would have got through. I think it was just a slice with the blade, not driven in like . . . like . . . ' She faltered, seeing that seeping pool of blood again.

He pulled her close to his chest. 'Hush, love, don't think of it. Or if you do, think of it with relief.'

'Relief?'

'Relief that your sister is now free of a bad marriage. Also relief that I am not facing the gallows for his murder. I assure you if I could have got to him without compromising your safety I would have hit him so hard, life would have been extinct within moments.'

She had never heard him sound so deadly. Paradoxically, her heart swelled with love for him. 'Charles?' she said softly.

He made an inarticulate sound and pressed a hard kiss on her forehead. 'God help me, no one is ever going to lay a hand on you again.'

Which was all very satisfactory but, 'You do not need to sound quite so grim about it,' she said.

He gave an exasperated sigh. 'Verity, you are . . . '

'Yours,' she said simply, then glanced through the window. 'We are here.'

'So we are. Later.' And this time he did kiss her lips — just once and swiftly — before opening the carriage door and helping her carefully out.

20

The incongruousness of Godmama's pretty sitting room, with Mama, Mr Tweedie, Kitty and Ann discovered in the act of eating macaroons and drinking lemonade, made Verity flounder. It was worlds away from the gambling hell and Charles's desperate game, worlds away from the stinking street with Kitty's husband's blood seeping into the ground. For a moment she didn't know where she was or why she was there. 'I . . . ' she began

Charles was faster to recover. 'Mrs Eastwick, I am glad to see you and your daughter here and safe.'

Kitty gave a tremulous smile. 'Your friend came for us so quickly there was no chance to change my mind. I hope I have not forgotten anything important. When can we be away to Newmarket, please? Simon knows this address.'

Charles squeezed Verity's hand, then walked forward and took Kitty's. 'That need not trouble you any more,' he said in a gentle tone. 'I must inform you of your husband's death. He was stabbed in the street by an unknown assailant as we were taking him to Bow Street to face charges.'

Kitty's hand went to her breast. 'Simon is dead?' She reached for her daughter. 'Ann, do you hear that? Your father is dead.'

The little girl looked up from where she was sitting on a footstool next to her grandmother. She had the same wariness in her eyes that Kitty often displayed when talking of Captain Eastwick, wariness that should never be seen on a child's face. 'May I have my new doll back then? He took it.'

'Yes, my love, if the pawn shop still has it. Oh, I hardly know what I am saying. Can I fetch the rest of my possessions from Henrietta Street? I left everything as if we had only stepped out to do the marketing. There is not much. Two gowns, cooking pots, bed linen, Ann's clothes.' She caught her lip. 'If they are still there, that is. News travels fast in those streets. With Simon dead, the landlady may already have bolted the door against us and taken our possessions in lieu of rent.'

'Oh!' said Verity, galvanised. 'As he died, Captain Eastwick whispered '*Kit's book. Get him*'. No one heard but me. I do not know which book he meant.'

Kitty gave a short laugh. 'I have only one book. Anything else would be sold or pawned. I brought it with me. I told you, it never leaves me now.' Delving into her basket, she extracted a small sturdy book showing evidence of much use. 'It does not surprise me that he had no last words for me. Has he written a message on one of the pages, do you suppose? I have never noticed anything.'

'May I see?' Charles reached for *Domestic Cookery* and moved to the sofa, motioning for Verity to sit down next to him.

This caused a furore by exposing the slit in her gown and her bloodstained bandage. Verity waved away offers of help, refusing to be tended to until Charles had examined the book.

'Nonsense,' said her mother, and gave immediate orders for hot water and bandages.

Charles continued to turn the pages. After a pause during which Verity submitted to her mother's ministrations and suspected every person in the room was convinced they should be investigating the book for themselves, he said, 'Have these last pages always been so stiff?'

Kitty looked bewildered. 'I don't know. It is only advertisements for other books.' She threw Mrs Bowman a fond glance. 'I needed no others, so I never bothered reading that part.'

Charles looked directly at Mr Tweedie. 'Do you have your penknife, sir? The one with the very fine blade.'

He has found something, thought Verity and thrilled at the serious, intent look in his eyes.

Mr Tweedie was suddenly all attorney. 'I do indeed. Pass the book over. I wonder, could we clear the table a little? Yes, I think you are correct, Charles. The edges are gummed. An old device, but surprisingly effective.' He paused, penknife suspended in mid-air, looking joyfully boyish. 'Goodness me, the last time I did this we discovered the location of a priceless pearl *parure* inside.'

'You may,' muttered Kitty, 'be disappointed.'

Verity grinned at her, then thanked her mother. 'Thank you, Mama. That feels very much easier.'

'I should imagine it does. I suppose you will tell me how you sustained it eventually?'

'Later. Look, Mr Tweedie has found something.'

Working the knife delicately, Mr Tweedie separated the final two pages in the book. A thin sheet of paper fluttered out, covered with writing. He retrieved it from the table, adjusted his spectacles and read it aloud. 'This appears to be a memorandum, written by Captain Eastwick. It reads: *July 1810 — went into Suffolk on a commission for F. I was to extract a single payment (as is his custom and guarantee) of £500 from Mr B to hide Mr B's part in the hiring and shooting of Mr WL as if by highwaymen in the year 1797.*' As he said this, Mr Tweedie's dry tone faltered and his eyes met those of Verity's mother. A hand crept to her mouth.

Mr Tweedie returned his attention to the letter. '*This is how F works. Money for a secret, paid once and for all time forgotten. Ten guineas for me as the agent, and the favour cancels out a secret he has on me. What else I do is my business, not his, though he frequently discovers it and holds the knowledge against me for a future task. He has spies everywhere. Whilst in Suffolk, I was much taken with Miss B. Her beauty and passion were beyond*

366

tempting. Mr B saw the attraction between us and offered £1000 for me in addition to F's payment if I would marry her & cause it to seem an elopement. To have £1000 plus my ten guineas for F's commission was a powerful inducement. I had often been paid to vacate the field, but never to marry. The deal was half down, proof to attorney, the remaining money paid on receipt. We were never to return to Newmarket. The lines are with Messrs D&D. I write this to affirm it was a true marriage and the way of it coming about. Signed by my hand . . . Simon Eastwick.'

Verity looked at Charles. 'What does it mean?'

'It means,' said Kitty in a bitter voice, 'that he never loved me. He was *paid* to run away with me so Papa should not have the expense of a wedding. I am so many times a fool.'

'It is more than that,' said Charles. 'From some papers we . . . acquired,' his gaze rested on Verity, 'your father's whole objective was to give your share of your late mother's settlement to your brother. He evidently thought the loss of a thousand pounds for a marriage bribe a sufficient price to pay for the gain of two. A despicable act in a father.'

'He was a monster.' Verity's mother spoke for the first time. There were tears in her eyes. 'He looked well enough, but he wasn't charming like your Simon, Kitty. I had no wish to wed him. Once Will died, I didn't think I had a choice. And now . . . now I find . . . ' Her voice shook with emotion. She put out a hand and — to Verity's shock — Mr Tweedie took it.

'Now we find Mr Bowman planned William Lawrence's death.' Mr Tweedie tapped the first part of the letter. 'That's what this says, that Mr Bowman was being blackmailed for hiring a ruffian to murder Will. He can only have done it to marry Miss Harrington, as she was in those days.'

'But why?' Verity was open-mouthed.

'I don't mean why would anyone want to marry you, Mama, for that is self-evident. But to kill your betrothed so *he* could marry you . . . that seems out-of-proportion pig-headed, even for Papa.'

'What he wanted, he got,' said her mother bleakly. 'He had decided on me for a second wife. I wasn't interested. So he removed his rival.'

'You were the most beautiful woman in the county,' said Mr Tweedie. 'Anyone would have fallen in love with you. I know I did.'

'Oh George, you are so sweet, but Mr Bowman didn't love me. He wanted to possess me. He played on my feelings by saying his two children needed a mother, then wouldn't let me spend time with them when I should have been attending to him. He demanded my compliance and beat me to make his point. After the first time, I was shocked and terrified into obedience. I couldn't leave him, I had nowhere else to go for my parents would simply have

369

returned me to Kennet End.' She smiled tremulously at Kitty. 'And I should have had to leave Kitty behind. I would never have been able to do that.'

Tears were running down Verity's sister's cheeks. 'And I repaid you by running away.'

'Hush, you were mine for thirteen years, and at the time we thought you were running from Mr Prout. That must have been another of his machinations — to force you to go.'

'I wish Papa had not been my father,' said Verity fiercely.

Mama exchanged a glance with Mr Tweedie. 'He wasn't,' she said composedly.

Verity was not the only person in the room who looked at her in amazement.

'George knows this, but I have never told another soul, though I believe my mother guessed and it was why she married me off so fast. Will and I were very much in love and so young that we knew we had a wondrous happy life in front of us. We anticipated the wedding as many couples have done before. I can never be sad about that, for it gave me the memory of that joy to sustain me. It gave me the knowledge of how love should be. And you, Verity. It gave me you.'

While Verity was still reeling — and revelling — in this knowledge, Mr Tweedie polished his spectacles and cleared his throat.

'I believe this might be an appropriate moment to announce that Mrs Bowman has done me the very, very great honour of agreeing to become my wife. I have no confidence in the sort of husband I will make, never having been one before, but I do know my only object is to make my dear Anne happy for the rest of her life.'

He was looking so anxious, but proud at the same time, that Verity immediately sprung up and embraced her mother. 'Oh, Mama, I am so pleased. I said if you married again it should be to someone who adored you and I can see this is the case. My goodness, Julia will be outraged to have missed all this when she and Godmama return.' She then embraced Mr Tweedie for good measure, from which he emerged looking even pinker.

'We are to live in the Kensington villa,' said her mother. 'George does not at all object to the longer journey to the Temple. I hope to prevail upon Cook and the others to come with us as I do not think they will want to stay in the dower house with whoever John rents it out to. I am afraid it ruins your plans for Furze House.'

Charles spoke. 'Not necessarily. First, may I wish you both every happiness. Secondly, with regard to Furze House, we have often said, have we not, sir, that it would be advantageous to have a base in Newmarket, as we have so many Suffolk clients. I have associates who are willing to take a share in the expenses of the house for the convenience of having somewhere to stay in the town. I also believe, very strongly, that Mrs Eastwick should not remain in London. Until we unravel more of her late husband's affairs, I cannot deem it safe for her here.' He tapped the memorandum. 'This statement shows clearly to me that the 'F' Captain Eastwick refers to had reason and more not to trust him in the hands of the magistrates. I believe it is he who had your husband killed, Kitty. You must not go back to Henrietta Street. Nor must you attempt to retrieve your possessions. He may well be watching and try to silence you as well, in case you were in your husband's confidence. My friend who brought you here is to travel to Newmarket for the racing tomorrow. I propose he leaves tonight and takes you and Ann with him. It is the last meeting of the season, so half the *ton* will be on the Newmarket Road. It will not be thought strange for Nicholas to be among them. Furze House is ready for possession though I cannot answer for the state of it.'

Kitty had grown so pale while

Charles was talking that Verity moved across and held her hand. 'Then please send him word,' said Kitty. 'I do not wish to remain in London. I should like nothing more than to return to Newmarket with Ann and bring her up safely away from all this.' She swallowed. 'But Simon had debts, I have no money . . . '

'His debts died with him,' said Charles. 'You are a free woman. As to money, I hope you will not take this amiss, but certainly in the first instance, we will need someone of experience and good character to run Furze House, someone who will be flexible about Verity's irregular proposal for it as a communal endeavour. Would you consider taking on this role for an annual allowance?'

Kitty's face lit up. 'I would be your housekeeper in effect? Yes — oh a thousand times, yes. If there is one thing I have learnt over the past seven years it is how to make a small budget stretch to unbelievable lengths.'

'It will not be as small as all that,' said Charles.

Verity applauded and hugged her sister, but uppermost in her mind as the others rushed off to assemble travelling bags and raid household equipment was just one question. *What of me?*

Charles, however, did not seem to be thinking of her at all. He wrote a swift note for his friend, gave it to a footman to deliver, then picked up the memorandum and frowned over it.

'What is it?' She asked in a low voice. 'Is it what he writes of 'F'?' She patted the cushion for Charles to sit next to her.

'Yes.' He looked troubled. 'This shows Eastwick was in some way bound to him, not just seven years ago, but also now. I have not forgotten your observation about how he knew of the heiresses. Suppose the information was given to him as one of these 'secrets' as he calls them? Such a man has a broad reach. If he is the same one I am thinking of, we have run across mention of him before. He exists in the shadows and as quickly vanishes when we look for him. I hope I did not alarm your sister too much but it is essential she travels tonight and stops for nothing on the way.'

Verity shivered. 'I believe she understands the danger. What of you? Won't you also be a target?'

'I do not think so. If he had spies inside that God-forsaken hell, they will tell him all Eastwick and I did was to play cards.'

'And me?' asked Verity.

'You,' said Charles, 'are not leaving my side. I have no right to ask you, and I do not know how we will manage, but I cannot live without you and I am done with being noble about leaving the field clear for some better man to rescue you from disasters and look after you.' He took her hands. 'I want you to know that this is not in any way a rational proposal, Verity. It is not because with our combined incomes we can run a house. It is not because half the militia in London and all of the hackney carriage drivers believe us to be already married and it would be more than I am capable of to enlighten them. It is not even because my senior partner sees nothing untoward in marrying a lady of quality, so there is no reason for me to hold back either.'

A great surge of hope filled Verity. 'No?'

'No. It is because I love you to distraction. I do not believe I will ever get another stroke of work done if you do not agree to plague my life on a daily basis and keep me in suspense about whatever madcap scheme you have embroiled us in this time. It is because I cannot let you go. Will you be my wife, Verity?'

Verity's whole being exploded with joy. 'Dearest Charles, of course I will. It is just a little vexing that I will not now be able to use any of the plans I had to compromise us so you *had* to offer for me, but it will be such an excellent adventure that I shall put the disappointment aside. How soon may we be married, please?'

'With as much dispatch as I can arrange. Meanwhile I will sleep here, I think. I shall not rest unless I know you are safe.'

'And you must tell all to Lord Fitzgilbert, I apprehend. Should we put it about that I am injured, so he conducts Lilith here to visit me on my sickbed?'

'You *are* injured. You should see a doctor.'

'Sit down. I will allow you to send for a doctor. I will not allow you to let go of my hand. What did Mama mean when she said she and my real father anticipated the marriage?'

Charles smiled in a way that turned her bones to water. 'I believe I mentioned you were not leaving my side, did I not? Later tonight I will come along to your room and show you.'

'And will you finally kiss me properly?'

Charles put an arm around her shoulders and brought her lips to meet his. 'Properly, improperly, and all the stages in between.'

Acknowledgements

Any mistakes are my own, but I owe particular thanks to Louise Allen, for not only being the best beta-reader and sounding board for Regency ideas in the world, but also for writing *Walking Jane Austen's London* and *Walks Through Regency London*, both of which have an extraordinary wealth of wonderful and useful information.

https://www.louiseallenregency.co.uk/

Ken Titmuss, alias the @oldmapman — https://oldparishmapwalks.wordpress.com — for his delightful walks with old maps, particularly the Soho and Covent Garden ones, the large-scale maps of which have been living on my desk for the past four months. And you, if I've forgotten to include you.